TOUCHÉ!

The party of Italian Communists was crossing the Russian border and no one except Peppone knew "Comrade" Camillo's real identity.

"At least we won't see any priests for two weeks," said Comrade Scamoggia.

"Comrade" Camillo shook his head. "Don't be too sure, Comrade," he said. "In the Soviet Union there's freedom of religion."

"You mean there are priests there too?"

Peppone said pointedly: "They will die out when poverty and ignorance are gone."

"That sounds like a personal prejudice, Comrade Peppone," Camillo said wryly.

Before the mayor could reply, toasts were proposed:

"To the Soviet Union!" roared Comrade Scamoggia.

"Down with capitalists!" rose the cry.

"Death to priests!" shouted Peppone, looking "Comrade" Camillo in the eye.

As the priest raised his cup, he gave Peppone an eloquent kick in the shins.

COMRADE DON CAMILLO
was originally published by
Farrar, Straus and Company.

COMRADE
DON CAMILLO

Giovanni Guareschi

Translated by Frances Frenaye

*Light reading —
but entertaining —
relaxing — Don't return*

A POCKET CARDINAL® EDITION published by
POCKET BOOKS, INC. • **NEW YORK**

COMRADE DON CAMILLO

Farrar, Straus edition published April, 1964

A Pocket *Cardinal* edition
1st printing........February, 1965

This Pocket *Cardinal*® edition includes every word contained in the
original, higher-priced edition. It is printed from brand-new
plates made from completely reset, clear, easy-to-read type.
Pocket *Cardinal* editions are published by Pocket Books, Inc.,
and are printed and distributed in the U.S.A. by Affiliated Publishers,
a division of Pocket Books, Inc., 630 Fifth Avenue, New York, N.Y. 10020.
Trademarks registered in the United States and other countries.

L

Contents

COMRADE DON CAMILLO

1

Gold Fever

THE NEWS exploded like a bomb around Monday noon, upon the arrival of the newspapers. Someone in the village had won ten million liras in the national soccer sweepstakes. The papers gave the name of the winner as Pepito Sbezzeguti, but no one in the town was known under such an exotic name. The bet collector, besieged by a curious mob, threw out his arms hopelessly.

"I sold any number of tickets to fellows from out of town at the market on Saturday," he said. "It must be one of them. Ten million liras! He's bound to show up."

But no one showed up, and the village continued to fret, because they felt sure there was something fishy about the name. Sbezzeguti was plausible, someone of that name might have come to the market. But Pepito was going a little too far. Nobody who dealt in wheat, corn, hay, livestock and Parmesan cheese would be called Pepito.

"It's a phoney name, if you ask me," said the proprietor of the Molinetto. "And someone using a false name isn't likely to be a stranger. It must be a villager who doesn't want it known that he played the sweeps. Maybe he doesn't want his debtors to know, or his wife."

The argument was logical enough. The villagers dropped the theory of the winner being an outsider and concentrated upon their fellow townsmen. They concentrated as

1

intently as if they were trying to identify a common thief rather than the winner of a legitimate pool.

Don Camillo followed the affair less passionately but with a certain amount of interest. And because he felt that Christ did not altogether approve of his leanings toward the trade of a detective he offered Him an explanation.

"Lord, it's not a matter of idle curiosity; I'm doing my duty. A man who has received such a favor from Divine Providence has no right to hide it."

"Don Camillo," replied Christ, "Divine Providence may take an interest in the soccer sweepstakes, although personally I doubt it, but surely not in all the publicity about the winnings. The fact of the matter is all that counts and it's quite adequately known. Someone has won a considerable sum of money, but why must you beat out your brains to discover his identity? Your business is to look after those who are less fortunate."

But Don Camillo couldn't rid himself of his curiosity. The mystery of Pepito continued to occupy his mind until finally a great light dawned upon him. It was all he could do not to ring the church bells in exultation, and quite beyond his powers to resist putting on his cloak and going for a walk in the village. In time he arrived at the workshop of Peppone, mayor and blacksmith. Don Camillo stuck his head through the door and greeted his enemy.

"Good morning, Comrade Pepito!"

Peppone stopped hammering and stared at the priest in dismay.

"What do you mean, Father?"

"Nothing at all. Pepito's a diminutive of Peppone, after all, and by some strange chance Sbezzeguti is an imperfect anagram of Giuseppe Bottazzi."

Peppone resumed his hammering.

Don Camillo shook his head.

"What a shame that you're not the Pepito who won the ten millions."

"A shame, yes. In that case I'd be able to offer you two or three millions to go back home."

"Don't worry, Peppone. I do favors for nothing," said Don Camillo, going away.

Two hours later the whole village knew what is meant by an anagram, and in every house Pepito Sbezzeguti was vivisected to find out if Comrade Giuseppe Bottazzi was lurking inside. That same evening the Reds' general staff held a special meeting at the People's Palace.

"Chief," said Smilzo, "the reactionaries have gone back to their old tactics of smearing a good name. The whole village is in an uproar. They say you won the ten millions. There's no time to be lost; you must nail down their slander."

Peppone threw out his arms.

"To say a fellow has won ten millions in the soccer sweepstake isn't slander. Slander means accusing someone of having done something dishonest, and the sweepstakes are quite on the level."

"Chief, in politics to accuse someone of a good deed is a smear. And an accusation that hurts the Party is definitely slanderous."

"People are laughing behind our backs," put in Brusco. "We've got to shut them up."

"We must print a poster!" Bigio exclaimed. "We must come up with a statement that makes everything clear."

Peppone shrugged his shoulders.

"We'll put our minds to it tomorrow," he said.

Whereupon Smilzo pulled a sheet of paper out of his pocket.

"We've something ready, Chief, in order to save you the trouble. If you approve we'll print it right away and paste up the posters tomorrow morning."

And he proceeded to read aloud:

The undersigned, Giuseppe Bottazzi, declares that he has

no connection with the Pepito Sbezzeguti who won ten million liras in the soccer sweepstakes. It is useless for the reactionaries to accuse him of being a millionaire. All it proves is that they are a gang of neo-Fascists.

　　　　　　　　　　　　　　　　—Giuseppe Bottazzi.

Peppone shook his head.

"It's all right," he said, "but until I see something in print I'm not going to rush into print myself with an answer."

But Smilzo stuck to his argument.

"Why wait to shoot until someone has shot at you? Good strategy calls for beating the opponent to the draw."

"Good strategy calls for a kick in the pants to anyone who sticks his nose into my private affairs. I can defend myself without help."

Smilzo shrugged his shoulders.

"If you take it like that, there's nothing more to say."

"That's how I do take it!" shouted Peppone, bringing his fist down on the table. "Every man for himself, and the Party for the lot of us!"

The general staff went away grumbling.

"To let himself be accused of having won ten million is a sign of weakness," observed Smilzo. "And besides, there's the complication of the anagram."

"Let's hope for the best," sighed Bigio.

Soon enough the rumor appeared in print. The landowners' paper published an insert that said: "*Scratch a Peppone and you'll find a Pepito*," and everyone in the village found this exceedingly clever and funny. The general staff held another meeting in the People's Palace and declared unanimously that something had to be done.

"Very good," said Peppone. "Go ahead and print the poster and paste it up."

Smilzo made a beeline for the printer's. Little more than

an hour later the printer, Barchini, brought Don Camillo a copy of the proofs.

"This is bad business for the newspaper," said Don Camillo sadly. "If Peppone really did win the money I don't think he would put out such a statement. That is, unless he's already gone to the city to collect it or sent someone else to collect it for him."

"He hasn't made a move," Barchini assured him. "Everyone in the village is on the alert."

It was late, and Don Camillo went to bed. But at three o'clock in the morning he was awakened by the news of a visit from Peppone. Peppone sneaked in from the garden, and when he was in the hall he peered out anxiously through the half-closed door.

"Here's hoping no one has seen me," he said. "I feel as if I were being followed."

Don Camillo glanced at him anxiously.

"You haven't gone crazy, have you?" he asked.

"No, no fear of that."

Peppone sat down and wiped the perspiration from his brow.

"Am I talking to the parish priest or to the village gossip?"

"That depends on what you came to say."

"I came to see the priest."

"The priest is listening," said Don Camillo gravely.

Peppone twirled his hat between his fingers and then confessed:

"Father, I told a big lie. I *am* Pepito Sbezzeguti."

For a moment Don Camillo was speechless.

"So you did win the millions, did you?" he said when he had recovered his aplomb. "Why didn't you say so?"

"I'm not saying so. I was speaking to you as a priest, and you should have no concern with anything but the fact that I told a lie."

But Don Camillo was concerned with the ten millions.

He shot a withering look at Peppone and moved to the attack.

"Shame on you! A proletarian, a Party member winning ten million liras in a soccer sweepstake! Leave such shenanigans to the bourgeoisie! Communists earn their living by the sweat of their brow."

"I'm in no mood for joking," gasped Peppone. "Is it a crime to place a bet in the soccer sweepstake?"

"It's no joke," said Don Camillo. "I didn't say it was a crime. I said that a good Communist wouldn't do it."

"Nonsense! Everyone does."

"That's very bad. And all the worse for you because you're a leader of the class struggle. The soccer sweepstake is a diabolical capitalist weapon turned against the People. Very effective, and it costs the capitalists nothing. In fact, they stand to make money. No good Communist can fail to combat it."

Peppone shrugged his shoulders in annoyance.

"Don't get excited, Comrade! It's all part of a vast conspiracy to persuade the proletariat to seek riches by other means than revolution. Of course that's pure fraud, and by abetting it you're betraying the cause of the People!"

Peppone waved his arms wildly.

"Father, let's leave politics out of it!"

"What's that, Comrade? Are you forgetful of the revolution?"

Peppone stamped his feet, and Don Camillo smiled indulgently.

"I understand, Comrade," he said, "and I don't blame you. Better ten million liras today than the revolution tomorrow!"

He went to poke up the fire and then turned around to look at Peppone.

"Did you come here just to tell me you'd won the money?"

Peppone was in a cold sweat.

"How can I get the cash without anyone's knowing?" he asked.

"Go for it, that's all."

"I can't. They're watching me like hawks. And besides my denial is coming out tomorrow."

"Then send a trusted comrade."

"There's no one I can trust."

"I don't know what to say," said Don Camillo, shaking his head.

Peppone held out an envelope.

"You go for me, Father."

He got up and went away, leaving Don Camillo to stare at the envelope.

The next morning Don Camillo set out for the city. Three days later he made his return. He arrived late in the evening, and before going to the rectory went to talk to the Christ over the altar. Opening up his suitcase he said sternly:

"Jesus, here are ten bundles, each one of them containing a hundred ten-thousand lira notes. In other words, the ten million liras that belong to Peppone. All I have to say is this: he doesn't deserve them."

"Tell that to the sweepstake operators," Christ replied.

Don Camillo took the suitcase away. When he reached the second floor of the rectory he switched the light on and off three times in succession as a signal to Peppone. Peppone replied by means of the light in his bedroom. Two hours later he arrived at the rectory, with his coat collar turned up to hide his face. He came in from the garden, through the door with the heavy padlock hanging from it.

"Well, then?" he said to Don Camillo, who was waiting in the pantry.

Don Camillo pointed at the suitcase, which was lying on the table, and Peppone approached it with trembling hands. When he saw the bundles of banknotes he broke into perspiration.

"Ten million?" he whispered questioningly.

"Ten million cold. Count them for yourself."

"Oh no," demurred Peppone, staring fascinatedly at the money.

"A pretty pile," commented Don Camillo, "at least for today. Who knows what it may be worth tomorrow? A single piece of bad news is enough to bring on inflation and turn it into worthless paper."

"I ought to invest it right away," said Peppone. "With ten millions I could buy a farm, and land always has value."

"It's the peasants that have a right to the land," said Don Camillo. "At least that's what the Communists say. They don't mention blacksmiths. They'll take it away from you, you'll see. Communism is the wave of the future, Comrade. . . ."

Peppone was still staring at the banknotes.

"I have it!" he exclaimed. "Gold! I'll buy gold and hide it away."

"What good will it do you? If the Communists take over, everything will come under the control of the State and your gold will lose its purchasing power."

"I could always deposit it abroad."

"Tut, tut! Like a regular capitalist! You'd deposit it in America, I suppose, because Europe is going Communist for sure. But when America is left out on a limb it will have to surrender to the Soviet Union."

"America's got real power," said Peppone. "The Soviet will never take it over."

"I wouldn't be so sure, Comrade."

Peppone took a deep breath and sat down.

"My head's whirling, Father. Ten million liras."

"Please oblige me by taking them home. But don't forget to send back my suitcase. That's my private property."

"No, Father," said Peppone. "Keep the money for me, will you? I'd rather talk about it when I can think straight, perhaps tomorrow."

After Peppone had gone away Don Camillo carried the suitcase up to his bedroom and went to bed. He was dead tired, but his sleep was interrupted at two o'clock in the morning by the reappearance of Peppone, together with his wife, both of them swathed in heavy coats.

"Forgive me, Father," said Peppone. "My wife just had to take a squint at the money."

Don Camillo brought down the suitcase and deposited it on the pantry table. At the sight of the banknotes Peppone's wife turned deathly pale. Don Camillo waited patiently, then he closed the suitcase and escorted the two of them to the door.

"Try to get some sleep," he said as they went away.

He tried to do the same thing himself, but an hour later he was once more awakened by Peppone.

"What's this?" he protested. "Isn't the pilgrimage over?"

"I came to take the suitcase," explained Peppone.

"Nothing doing! I've stowed it away in the attic and I have no intention of bringing it down. You can come back tomorrow. I'm cold and tired and entitled to my rest. Don't you trust me?"

"It's not a question of trust. What if something were to happen to you during the night? How could I prove that the money is mine?"

"Don't worry about that. The suitcase is locked and there's a tag with your name on it. I've thought of every contingency."

"I appreciate that, Father. But the money's safer in my house."

Don Camillo didn't like his tone of voice. And he changed his own to match it.

"What money are you talking about?"

"My own! The money you went to get for me in Rome."

"You must be crazy, Peppone. I never got any of your money."

"The ticket's in my name," shouted Peppone. "I'm Pepito Sbezzeguti."

"It's plastered all over the walls that you're *not* Pepito Sbezzeguti. You signed the statement yourself."

"I am, though! Pepito Sbezzeguti is an anagram of Giuseppe Bottazzi."

"No it isn't. It's an anagram of Giuseppe Bottezzi. I have an uncle of that name and it's for him that I cashed in the ticket."

With a trembling hand Peppone wrote *Pepito Sbezzeguti* on the margin of the newspaper lying on the table, and after it his real name.

"Damnation!" he exclaimed. "I put an *e* for an *a*. But the money's mine."

Don Camillo started up the stairs to his bedroom, with Peppone following after.

"Don't take it so hard, Comrade," he called out as he climbed into bed. "I won't steal your money. I'll use it for your own cause, for the cause of the downtrodden people."

"Devil take the people!" Peppone shouted.

"You benighted reactionary!" said Don Camillo, pulling the sheet up over his head. "Go away and let me sleep!"

"Give me my money, or I'll kill you like a dog!"

"Take the filthy stuff and go away!"

The suitcase was on the chest of drawers. Peppone seized it, hid it under his coat and ran down the stairs.

When Don Camillo heard the front door slam he gave a deep sigh.

"Lord," he said sternly, "why did you let him ruin his life by winning that money? He doesn't deserve such punishment."

"First you scold me because he didn't deserve such a

prize and now you call it a punishment! I can't seem to please you, Don Camillo!"

"I wasn't talking to you, Lord; I was talking to the sweepstake operators," Don Camillo murmured as he finally fell asleep.

2

Don Camillo's Revenge

Lord," SAID DON CAMILLO, "he's gone a bit too far, and I shall destroy him!"

"Don Camillo," said the crucified Christ over the altar, "they went a bit too far when they hung me up on this Cross, but I managed to forgive them."

"But they didn't know what they were doing! Peppone had his eyes wide open and deserves no pity."

"Look here, Don Camillo," Christ retorted; "ever since Peppone became a senator haven't you been particularly hard on him?"

These words hit home, and Don Camillo resented them.

"You wouldn't say that, Lord," he protested, "if you knew me a little better."

"Oh, I know you well enough," Christ sighed in reply.

Don Camillo knew when to stop. He hastily bent one knee, crossed himself and glided away. But outside the church his resentment was reawakened. Just beside the rectory door some unfortunate fellow had just pasted up a copy of the poster which had aroused his original anger. It was a story that dated back to two years before.

One gloomy winter evening, when Don Camillo was just about to go to bed, someone had knocked at the rectory door. Don Camillo saw that of course it was Peppone. He motioned him to a chair and handed him a glass of wine, which Peppone drained with a single gulp. It took two more glasses to loosen his tongue, and then he came out with:

"I can't stand it!"

From under his heavy black cape he pulled out a bundle.

"Ever since I've had this in the house I haven't been able to sleep."

It was the famous ten million liras, of course, and Don Camillo replied:

"Then put it in the bank."

Peppone gave a wry laugh.

"That's a very poor joke! How can a Communist mayor deposit ten million liras in the bank without saying where he got them?"

"Convert them into gold and bury it in the ground!"

"That way I wouldn't get any interest on my capital."

Don Camillo was sleepy, but his patience was not yet exhausted.

"Come along, Comrade," he said pacifically; "let's get to the point."

"Well then, Father, you know that businessman who takes such good care of other people's money. . . ."

"No, I don't know him."

"Surely you do. He belongs to your camp. A fellow that gets a lot of business from church people and then eases his conscience with big donations to religious charities. . . ."

"Oh yes, I have an idea whom you mean. But I've never had any dealings with him."

"But you can get in touch with him very easily. The priest at Torricella is one of his agents."

Don Camillo wearily shook his head.

"Comrade," he said, "just because God gave you an inch, do you have to take a mile?"

"God has nothing to do with it, Father. I had a stroke of good luck and now I want to take advantage of it."

"Then it's perfectly simple. Go to the priest at Torricella and ask him for an introduction."

"No, I can't do that. People know my face too well. If they were to see me hanging around the rectory at Torricella or the businessman's office, I'd lose my reputation. Imagine a Communist getting mixed up with the Church and high finance! If I can keep my name out of it, then it's strictly a matter of money. I can't let it become a political football."

Don Camillo had always taken a dim view of the businessman who earned sky-high interest rates for his clients and then contributed to the building of new churches. But the Torricella priest was a thoroughly decent fellow and if he had acquired a sports field, a swimming pool, a moving-picture projector and other attractions to compete with those offered by the Reds, it was all thanks to the generosity of this wealthy parishioner. And so Don Camillo suspended his judgment.

"I don't want to get myself involved in any more complications," he said. "Tomorrow evening at this time, I'll arrange to have the priest come over from Torricella. I'll go to bed and leave you to talk with him."

Twenty-four hours later Peppone and the other priest met in Don Camillo's study. They seemed to have reached some agreement, for Don Camillo heard no more of the affair. A year later Peppone was elected to the Senate, and from then on Don Camillo was besieged by some devil.

"Peppone is an ingrate," the devil whispered in his ear. "You were a good friend to him when you went to collect the sweepstakes money, and what has he done for you in return? No sooner was he elected than he made an inflammatory speech in the pubic square."

Portions of the inflammatory speech had been brought to Don Camillo's attention. In boasting of his electoral triumph Peppone had made scathing references to *a certain priest who used all sorts of pious platitudes to prevent a*

victory of the People, a priest who would better be em-
ployed as a bell ringer if only he knew how to ring a bell."
Quite obviously Don Camillo was tempted to retaliate by
telling the story of Peppone's clandestine sweepstakes winnings.

For two whole years the priest staved off this temptation.
He had just about banished it from his mind when he saw
the new Communist poster. Just at that time the famous
businessman had got his name into the headlines as the
central figure of a financial scandal. When the scandal was
at its height, Peppone launched this attack against him, in
which he included *"certain conniving priests who, for love*
of money, did not hesitate to join hands with a notorious
swindler in order to rob the faithful of their hard-earned
savings."

This shameless accusation was more than Don Camillo
could take, and he made up his mind to explode a little
bomb of his own.

Peppone came back quite often to the village. He was
now a very different man, carrying a brief case full of state
papers and wearing a self-important and preoccupied air,
as if the affairs of the whole world weighed upon his shoulders. He greeted the local people distractedly and inspired
fear even among his Party comrades. Whenever anyone
brought him a problem he said solemnly: "I'll take it up in
Rome." He went in for dark, double-breasted suits and conventional felt hats and never appeared without a tie. The
poster contained glaring grammatical errors, but since his
personality was quite strong enough to overshadow his
style, no one dared make fun of them. Don Camillo laid his
plans and accosted him at eleven o'clock one night at the
door of his house.

"Excuse me," he said, while Peppone was turning the
key in the lock, "but do you happen to be one of the poor

innocents fleeced by conniving priests who joined hands with a notorious swindler?"

Peppone had succeeded in opening the door and now he had no choice but to let Don Camillo in. At once Don Camillo drove his point home.

"Comrade Senator," he went on, "the next trick is mine. When I tell the whole truth, you'll be the laughingstock of the whole country. Just wait until your electors find out that you cheated both the tax collector and the Communist Party of your sweepstakes winnings! And how you cheated them again by turning over your ten million liras to a criminal speculator, one of those whom you define as the Enemies of the People!"

Peppone threw out his chest defiantly.

"I'll sue you for libel," he retorted. "You can't prove a thing."

"I'll prove the whole story. Your name is in that man's files. He sent your interest payments by check, and I have the check numbers."

Peppone wiped a sudden access of perspiration from his brow.

"You'd never play me a dirty trick like that!"

Don Camillo sat down and lighted his cigar butt.

"It's no dirty trick," he said. "It's just a reply to your poster."

Peppone let himself go. He tore off his jacket and threw it onto a sofa and loosened his tie. Then he sat down directly across from Don Camillo.

"You don't need to take revenge," he groaned. "I lost every penny."

"But you'd been getting such exorbitant interest for the past two years that you pretty nearly came out even."

Peppone felt trapped, and in desperation he blurted out: "Father, will you settle for three million?"

"Comrade, you have no right to insult me with such an offer. That will cost you something extra."

He pulled out a newspaper, unfolded it and pointed out an article on one of the back pages.

"You see, Senator, we know what's going on. We see that you have been given the important job of picking ten deserving comrades whom you're to escort on a free tour of Soviet Russia. We shan't interfere with this project. But as soon as you've left the country we'll let the cat out of the bag. The embarrassment of your Party leaders will add to the fun."

Peppone was speechless. Knowing Don Camillo as he did, he realized that there was no chance of stopping him. His crumpled air moved the priest to compassion.

"Comrade," he said, "you can consider yourself liquidated. That is, unless. . . ."

"Unless what?" groaned Peppone, raising his head.

Quite calmly Don Camillo set forth the only means of escaping disgrace. Peppone listened with his jaw sagging.

"Father, you're joking," he said when the priest had finished.

"It's no joke. It's do or die."

"You're mad, Father," said Peppone, leaping to his feet. "Stark, raving mad!"

"Exactly, Comrade. That's why you'd better think twice before you say no. Madmen can be dangerous. I give you until tomorrow night."

Two days later Don Camillo went to the old Bishop who heard him out patiently to the end of his story.

"Is that all?" he inquired. "I think that with a rest cure in the mountains you may get over it."

Don Camillo shook his head.

"I meant every word," he insisted. "It's the opportunity of a lifetime. Two whole weeks of direct contact with a group of our most ardent Communists and also with the Russians! . . ."

The Bishop looked at him with dismay.

"My son, who put this idea into your head?"

"Nobody. It just came upon me. Who knows? Perhaps it was inspired by the Lord."

"I can't believe it," muttered the Bishop. "Anyhow, you're dead set upon it, and you expect me to let you go without breathing a word to a soul. What if they discover who you are?"

"They won't discover that, I promise you. I'll take pains to disguise myself. I don't mean so much by the clothes I wear as by my frame of mind. That's what really counts. A normal mind has to take on Communist processes of thought, if facial expression and tone of voice are to fit in with the Communist pattern."

The Bishop tapped his cane against the stool where he was resting his feet.

"It's sheer madness, my son," he concluded.

"Yes, Your Grace," agreed Don Camillo.

"But you may go," the Bishop added.

Don Camillo knelt down, and the Bishop laid a wasted hand on his bowed head.

"God be with you, Comrade Don Camillo," he said, raising his eyes to heaven.

He spoke in such a low voice that Don Camillo barely heard what he was saying. But God had no difficulty hearing.

3

Don Camillo in Disguise

GOOD MORNING, SENATOR," said the sharp-tongued cleaning woman who was scrubbing the boarding-house floor.

"Good morning, Comrade," cautiously murmured the milkman, who was just making his morning delivery.

"Good morning, you poor fool," said a stout-bodied man who was standing square in the middle of the sidewalk, waiting for him to come by.

Peppone did not deign to answer; he pushed him aside and went on his way. The scene was Rome, at nine o'clock in the morning. The vast machinery of the capital was slowly getting under way and a remnant of sleepiness still dulled the crisp freshness of the autumn air.

"Good morning, you poor fool," repeated the stout-bodied man, this time in a cordial, almost affectionate manner. "Up in the country this is the beginning of a wonderful day. Mist is rolling off the ploughed fields, the clover is shiny with dew and the vines are heavy with clusters of ripe, honey-sweet grapes, half-hidden by russet leaves. . . ."

Peppone grunted in reply. Did his enemy have to lie in ambush every morning in front of the boarding house and then buzz about him with the latest village news? To quiet his nerves he lit a cigarette.

"Of course," the other jeered. "A cigar would never do. City people don't like strong smells, and if your landlady were to see you with a cigar butt hanging out of one corner of your mouth, senators would go down in her esteem. A very nice old lady she is, by the way, and you did well to tell her you were an 'independent.' It would be quite a shock to her to find out that you're a Communist."

Peppone threw away his cigarette and loosened his tie.

"Yes, I know that you used to feel more comfortable with your shirt open and a handkerchief knotted around your neck. But a senator can't go around looking like a hayseed. You're a big shot now, with a telephone on your desk and marble tiles on your office floor."

Peppone glanced at his watch.

"Don't worry," said the voice beside him. "You're doing a very good job. You displayed excellent judgment in the choice of candidates for your Russian tour. Only one name is missing from the list."

Peppone took off his hat and wiped the perspiration from his forehead.

"It's all the fault of that speculator! I wish I'd never met him."

"Look here, my boy," said his interlocutor with genuine feeling, "you don't have to let yourself in for any of this. Why go looking for trouble? You can kick off the traces and come on home."

"No, I can't," groaned Peppone.

"Then good-by until tomorrow, and God help you!"

They had come to the bus stop, and Peppone watched his friendly enemy walk away and lose himself in the crowd. Did the fellow have to haunt him every morning with memories of the past, of days when he had been a simpler but happier man, to tease him with the siren call of "Home, Sweet Home"?

On the bus Peppone sat down across from a man who

was reading the Communist daily, *L'Unità del Popolo,* which he held wide open before him, as stiffly as if it were mounted on a wooden frame. Peppone could not see his fellow passenger's face, but this dramatically provocative pose convinced him that he must be a jackass. *"Every Party member should wear a Party emblem in his button-hole, but to display it ostentatiously is contrary to common sense."* So Peppone himself had decreed in the good old days, when someone had played a miserable, low-down trick on his dog, Thunder. Don Camillo had scolded Peppone for failing to take off his hat when the Blessed Sacrament went by, and Peppone had answered with insulting remarks. Shortly after this, Thunder had come home with all his hair shaved off, except on his rump, where it had been trimmed in the pattern of a hammer and sickle. And every time that Don Camillo met the dog, he tipped his hat in mock respect for the Party emblem.

"Those were the days," Peppone thought to himself, "before people were really bitten by the political bug and a good laugh straightened out their relationship better than any amount of bitter discussion."

The conventionally dressed man across the way lowered his paper and Peppone had to admit that he didn't look like a jackass. His eyes were expressionless, but this was doubtless because the thick lenses of his glasses concealed them from view. He was wearing a commonplace light suit and an even more commonplace gray hat. Somehow or other he was unpleasant, and Peppone was annoyed to see him get off at the same bus stop as himself.

"Sir," the man asked him, "can you show me the way to . . . ?"

Peppone lost all control.

"I can show you the way to go to hell," he shouted.

"Exactly what I wanted to know," said the man calmly.

Peppone strode rapidly away, and the other followed after. Five minutes later he sat down at the same isolated table in a small, empty café. After Peppone had cooled himself off with a heaping dish of ice cream he regained sufficient self-control to speak.

"Your bad joke has gone far enough," he decreed.

"Not a bit of it. This is only the beginning."

"You don't expect me to take you seriously, do you?"

"I not only expect it; I demand it."

"Now, Don Camillo—"

"Call me Comrade Tarocci. . . ." And he took a passport out of his pocket. "There it is, in black and white: 'Camillo Tarocci, linotypist.' "

Peppone turned the passport over and over in his hands, looking at it disgustedly.

"A false name, a false passport, false colors."

"No, Comrade, the passport is genuine. It was issued to Camillo Tarocci, linotypist, and I'm practically his spitting image. If you don't believe me, just look at this." And holding out a piece of paper, he explained: "Here you have a membership card of the Communist Party, issued to Camillo Tarocci. Everything's authentic and in good order." And before Peppone could interrupt him he went on: "There's nothing to be surprised about. Some of the comrades aren't what they seem. But since Tarocci is one of the star members of his cell, you have only to write and ask him for the names of half a dozen fellows particularly deserving to be taken along on your tour and then choose him instead. Then while he takes a fortnight's country vacation I'll tag along with you. I'll have a good look at Russia, and when I come back I'll tell him all about it."

It was all Peppone could do to keep his temper.

"I don't know or care whether there really is a hell," he spluttered. "But if there is one, that's where you're going."

"Then we shall meet again in the next life, Comrade."

At this point Peppone's defenses broke down.

"Father," he said wearily, "why are you dead set on destroying me?"

"Nobody's dead set on destroying you, Comrade. My presence on your Russian tour isn't going to affect the state of things in Russia. The good things will be good and the bad things will be bad whether I'm there or not. Why are you so nervous? Are you afraid it isn't the workers' paradise that your newspapers make it out to be?"

Peppone shrugged his shoulders.

"As far as I'm concerned," Don Camillo went on, "I'm hoping it isn't as bad as our papers paint it."

"Very fine feelings!" exclaimed Peppone sarcastically. "How objective and disinterested you are!"

"I'm not disinterested at all," Don Camillo retorted. "It's to my interest that the Russians should be happy. That way they'll stay quietly at home and not go bother other people."

A week later Comrade Camillo Tarocci received the news that he had been chosen to go on the Russian tour. Carrying a cheap suitcase he reported at the Communist Party headquarters, along with the nine other tour members. A young Party official received the little group introduced to him by the senator and issued terse parting instructions.

"Comrades, you have a definite mission to perform. You are to keep your eyes and ears open, not only on your own behalf but also on behalf of your comrades at home. When you come back you must tell friends and foes alike about the technical accomplishments and peaceful spirit of the glorious Soviet Union."

While Peppone visibly paled with apprehension, Don Camillo asked permission to make a statement.

"Comrade," he said, "it's hardly worthwhile to travel so far merely in order to come back and tell our friends something they already know and our foes something they refuse to admit. My idea is that our mission should be to convey to our Russian hosts the joyous and grateful greetings of the Italian people for their liberation from the threat of war."

"Of course, Comrade," muttered the Party official; "that goes without saying."

He went away, sticking out his chest and looking slightly annoyed, and Peppone turned ferociously on Don Camillo.

"When something goes without saying then it needn't be said. Besides, you must speak in a way that shows some respect for the person to whom you are speaking. Obviously you don't know who that was."

"Oh yes, I do," Don Camillo imperturbably replied. "He's a twenty-five-year-old young man, who was about ten when the war began. He never fought with us up in the mountains against the Germans and so he can't possibly know what a terrible thing war is or how psychologically important is Comrade Khrushchev's trip to America to forward the cause of peace and disarmament."

"Well spoken," said Comrade Nanni Scamoggia, a hulking fellow from the proletarian Trastevere section of Rome, with a tough and devil-may-care air about him. "When there's fighting to be done, you'll never see one of these Party big shots on the scene."

"And when these bureaucrats start setting up a bureaucracy . . ." added Comrade Walter Rondella, a workingman from Milan. But before he could say any more Peppone interrupted.

"We're not here to hold a meeting. If we don't step fast we'll miss the train."

He walked briskly toward the door, shooting Don Camillo an atomic glance loaded with enough power to topple a skyscraper. But Don Camillo preserved the stony expression of a comrade who, whatever the cost, will not deviate a single inch from the Party line.

On the train Peppone's chief preoccupation was not to

let the diabolical Comrade Camillo Tarocci out of his sight.
He sat directly in front of him in order to block his way.
But Don Camillo did not seem to be in a mood for making
trouble. He took out of his pocket a book with a red jacket
and a gold hammer and sickle stamped upon it and with
an impenetrable expression on his face immersed himself
in its perusal. At rare intervals he raised his eyes and
looked out at the fields and villages gliding by the train.
As he closed the book and started to put it back in his
pocket, Peppone remarked:

"Must be good reading."

"The very best," said Don Camillo. "It's a collection of
excerpts from Lenin." And he added, handing it over for
inspection: "Too bad it's in French. But I can translate any
part you'd like to hear."

"No thanks, Comrade," said Peppone, closing the book
and returning it to its owner.

He looked cautiously around him and breathed a sigh
of relief when he saw that all his other traveling companions were either dozing or turning the pages of illustrated magazines. No one had noticed that in spite of the
red jacket and the French title, *Pensées de Lénine*, the
book was actually a Latin breviary.

At the first stop several of the men got off the train.
Comrade Scamoggia came back with a bottle of wine and
Comrade Rondella with an extra of an evening newspaper,
over which he was shaking his head disgustedly. On the
front page there were pictures of Khrushchev's last day in
America and the usual crowd of smiling faces around him.

"I don't know what it is, but to see him smile in the company of those grinning mugs is more than I can stomach."

"Politics is a question of brains, not of feeling," said Don
Camillo. "The Soviet Union has been struggling all along
to achieve peaceful co-existence. The capitalists who
fostered the cold war are the ones who have very little to

smile about. The end of the cold war is a capitalist disaster."

But Rondella had all the obstinacy of the typical organized Milanese worker.

"That's all very well. But I have a perfect right to say that I hate capitalists and I'd rather be seen dead then caught smiling with them."

"You have a perfect right to say what you please. But don't say it to us; say it to Khrushchev. By the time we get to Moscow he'll be there. You can ask to see him and then say to his face: 'Comrade Khrushchev, you're on the wrong track.'"

Don Camillo was as sly as the slyest Communist secret agent. Comrade Rondella turned pale.

"Either you can't or you won't understand me," he protested. "If I have to handle manure in order to fertilize a field, then I'll handle it. But no one can force me to say that it has a good smell."

"Comrade," said Don Camillo quietly, "you fought with the Partisans, I know. When you were ordered into danger, what did you do?"

"I went."

"And did you tell your comrades that you couldn't stomach the idea of risking your life?"

"Of course not. But what's the connection?"

"War is war, Comrade, whether it's hot or cold. And the man who's fighting for a just cause can't afford to have opinions of his own."

"Drop it, Comrade Rondella," intervened Peppone. "We're going to a country where you won't run into any capitalists, that's one thing sure."

"And it makes me feel considerably better," admitted Rondella.

"The thing I'm happiest about," said Comrade Scamoggia, "is that for a whole fortnight we shan't run into any priests."

Don Camillo shook his head.

"I wouldn't be too certain about that, Comrade. In the Soviet Union there's freedom of religion."

"Freedom of religion? Ha! ha!" jeered Scamoggia.

"Don't laugh! The Soviet Union takes its freedom seriously."

"You mean there are priests there too? Does that filthy breed really defy extermination?"

"It will die out of its own accord, when poverty and ignorance are gone," put in Peppone. "Poverty and ignorance are meat and drink to those black crows."

But Don Camillo was colder and more severe than ever.

"Comrade Senator, you know better than I that in the Soviet Union poverty and ignorance have been done away with already. If there are still priests, it can only be because they have some power which there is as yet no way to overcome."

"What *have* they got?" Scamoggia shouted. "Aren't they made of flesh and blood, like ourselves?"

"No!" shouted back Peppone. "They're the dregs of the earth! They're a band of cowards, hypocrites, blackmailers, thieves and assassins! Even a poisonous snake will go out of his way to avoid a priest, for fear of being bitten."

"You're going overboard, Comrade Senator," said Don Camillo. "Your violence must be based on something personal. Tell me, did some priests do you dirt?"

"The priest's yet to be born that can do me dirt!" protested Peppone.

"What about the priest that baptized you?"

"I was only one day old!"

"And the priest that married you?" Don Camillo insisted.

"Don't argue with him, Chief," laughed Scamoggia. "This comrade is the dialectical, hair-splitting type; he'll always have the last word."

And he added, turning to Don Camillo:

"Comrade, you're a man after my own heart! You know what you're talking about and you hate the priests just as much as I do."

He poured wine into the paper cups and proposed a toast:

"To the Soviet Union!"

"Down with capitalists!" said Comrade Rondella.

"Death to priests!" roared Peppone, looking Don Camillo straight in the eye.

As Don Camillo raised his cup he gave Peppone an eloquent kick in the shins.

It was midnight when the train reached the frontier. The moon was full, bathing in its light the villages perched among the mountains. Every now and then the travelers caught a glimpse of the plains below, with rivers running like ribbons across them and cities that were clusters of sparkling lights. Don Camillo stood at one of the corridor windows, puffing at his cigar butt and enjoying the sight. Peppone came to stand beside him, and after gazing at length out the window heaved a deep sigh.

"You can say what you like, but when a man is about to leave his country he suddenly appreciates it."

"Comrade, you're indulging in outworn rhetoric and nationalism. Don't forget that our country is the world."

"Well then, why do so many poor fools want to go to the moon?" Peppone asked without thinking.

"Comrade, something distracted my attention, and I didn't hear your question."

"It's just as well you didn't," mumbled Peppone.

4
Operation Rondella

THE TRI-MOTOR PLANE on which the little group embarked at an airport in East Germany was so noisy that no one could make his voice heard above the din. Comrade Don Camillo was forced to hold his tongue and Peppone enjoyed relative peace of mind. Nevertheless he remained alert, for Don Camillo was a dangerous character even when he was silent. For the moment he was confining his anti-Communist activities to reading the supposed excerpts from the works of Lenin, and Peppone had no cause for worry until the priest closed the book and smote his forehead with one hand, as if he had just had a bright idea. But he quickly neutralized the effect of this alarming gesture by stroking his hair and then dusting off the lapels of his jacket.

"Amen," muttered Peppone with a deep sigh, which cleared his sputtering carburetor. The plane was gradually losing altitude and soon put down its wheels on Soviet soil.

"Lord, my little church seems very far away!" Don Camillo thought as he went down the waiting steps.

"But Heaven is very near," the Lord reassured him.

Don Camillo pulled himself together and resumed the role of Comrade Tarocci.

"Comrade," he said gravely to Peppone, "don't you feel an urge to pick up a clod of this sacred earth and kiss it?"

"Yes, and after that to ram it down your throat," Peppone muttered between clenched teeth.

Notice had been received of the visitors' arrival, and a girl stepped forward to meet them, followed by a man in a flapping, faded raincoat.

"Greetings, Comrades!" she said brightly. "I am Nadia Petrovna, your interpreter, and this is Yenka Oregov from the government tourist bureau."

She spoke excellent Italian, and if it hadn't been for her fixed stare and the severity of her tailored suit, she might have been a girl from our own part of the world.

Peppone introduced himself and his companions, and after an orgy of handshaking the tourist-bureau official made a little speech welcoming them in the name of their Soviet brothers, co-fighters for the cause of freedom, social justice and peace. He was a stocky fellow, some forty years old, with a shaven head, a square jaw, thin lips, darting eyes and a bull neck. Standing there in the raincoat that came almost down to his ankles, he had the unmistakable air of a policeman. He spoke without moving the muscles of his face and with such wooden gestures that if his speech had not been translated to them they might have taken it for a prosecutor's harangue rather than a welcome. Comrade Nadia Petrovna affected the same official stiffness, but there was something definitely softer about her.

Comrade Nanni Scamoggia was struck dumb, although she was by no means the first pretty girl he had seen in the course of his heartbreaker's career. He was twenty-eight years old and every inch a Roman, with shiny, black, wavy hair, eyes that had a slightly perverse expression and long lashes, an ironical twist to his lips, broad shoulders, narrow hips and feet as small as a ballet dancer's. He wore tight-fitting trousers, a red shirt and a black leather jacket, and a cigarette drooped out of one corner of his mouth. He was half tough, half dandy, quick to use his fists and accustomed to having his way with women.

As the little group crossed the airfield, with Peppone, Comrade Oregov and Comrade Nadia Petrovna leading the way, Scamoggia regained his power of speech.

"Comrade," he said to Don Camillo, "how's *she* for an atom bomb? Do you find her as easy on the eyes as I do?"

"I do," answered Don Camillo, mentally asking the Lord's indulgence. "They don't make girls any prettier than that one."

He spoke loudly, for the benefit of Comrade Rondella, who promptly rose to the bait.

"She's pretty enough," he admitted, "but we've got just as pretty girls at home."

"At home they know how to dress," said Don Camillo. "But put one of them into the clothes Comrade Petrovna is wearing and she'd cut a very poor figure. This girl has real classical beauty; she's not just one of those dolls you see in our cities. Especially in Milan, where they're born knowing all the answers."

"Nonsense, Comrade!" protested Rondella. "There are girls in Milan as pretty as you could hope to see."

"Cool off, Comrade," intervened Scamoggia. "We've got pretty girls, all right, but this one has something special. I can't put my finger on it, but it's there."

"It depends on the environment in which she was brought up. It's environment that shapes the man, and also the woman. This is an elementary truth, but plenty of people don't seem to understand it."

Comrade Rondella had another two cents' worth to put in, but a sudden halt interrupted him.

"Customs inspection," announced Peppone, threading his way back among them. And he added, in Don Camillo's ear: "I hope you aren't carrying anything that will get us into hot water."

"Comrade," said Don Camillo reassuringly, "I know the ways of the world."

The inspection was quickly over, because Peppone had

made efficient preparations for it. Every member of the
group had the same type of cheap suitcase and all the
contents had identical weight. The only thing that gave
any trouble was a bottle in the possession of Scamoggia.
The customs inspector unscrewed the top, sniffed at the
liquid inside and then handed it over to be sniffed by
Comrade Petrovna.

"He wants to know why you're carrying a woman's
perfume," she explained.

"It isn't a woman's perfume," Scamoggia told her. "It's
eau-de-cologne for after shaving. What sort of lotion do
they have around here? Gasoline?"

She started to reply, but she could see that a fellow as
tough-looking as this one wasn't to be put in his place so
easily. And so she contented herself with translating only
the first part of his statement. The inspector muttered
something unintelligible and put the bottle back in the
suitcase.

"Here they have pure alcohol," she informed Scamoggia.
"He says you can keep it for your own personal use, but
you're not to sell it."

After they had left the field Scamoggia stopped and
reopened his suitcase.

"Wait a minute," he said. "If it's the custom here for
men to use pure alcohol, then I'll follow their example.
Since this is considered a woman's perfume, then a woman
should have it."

He started to give her the bottle, but she drew her hand
away.

"Aren't you a woman?" asked Scamoggia.

"Of course," she stammered.

"Then take it. I'm not putting it up for sale; it's a present."

She seemed perplexed, but finally she took the bottle and
stowed it away in the bag swinging from her shoulder.

"Thank you, Comrade," she managed to say.

"You're welcome, good-looking!"

Comrade Petrovna tried to give him a haughty bureaucratic stare but succeeded only in blushing like a little capitalist. She ran to catch up with the rest of the party, while Scamoggia closed his suitcase, lit a cigarette and let it dangle from one corner of his mouth, with an air of obvious satisfaction.

A bus was waiting for them, and they climbed in. As Peppone was hoisting his suitcase onto a shelf above the seats Don Camillo tapped him on the shoulder.

"Chief," he said, "there must be some sort of mix-up. I seem to have your suitcase."

Peppone examined the tag and saw that it was indeed his. He took the other one down from the shelf and sure enough it was tagged with the name of Camillo Tarocci.

"Nothing serious," said Don Camillo. "Just as I said, it's a mix-up."

Peppone sat down, across from Don Camillo. After the bus had started a second thought crossed his mind.

"So when we went through the customs I was carrying your suitcase," he said.

"Accidentally, you were."

"And accidentally did your suitcase have something contraband in it?"

"Oh, nothing much. A few holy cards, a picture of the Pope and some communion wafers."

Peppone shuddered all over.

The bus was traveling through an endless expanse of flat country, where scrawny cows were grazing on the meager autumnal grass. Comrade Petrovna announced that they were going to visit a tractor factory, after which they would be taken to a hotel for dinner and a night's rest.

The factory was on the outskirts of the city of R. It was an agglomeration of dismal gray cement buildings rising abruptly out of the plains to the north.

"This ugliness is the product of what's called an 'industrial civilization,' and it's the same the world over," Don Camillo thought mournfully to himself, feeling acutely homesick for his faraway village, where every brick had been put in place by a man's hand and men and things were bound by invisible ties together.

The workers wore the indifferent, bored air common to their kind. Some parts of the factory were staffed exclusively by women, stocky little creatures who did not in the least resemble Comrade Petrovna. At a certain point Comrade Rondella could not help edging up to Don Camillo and saying:

"Comrade, these women don't look as if they'd grown up in the same favorable environment as our charming interpreter!"

Don Camillo made a shattering reply.

"Comrade, you can't look at women factory workers as if they were contestants in a beauty parade! Every self-respecting Communist knows that."

It was no time for an argument, especially as Peppone was shooting dagger looks in their direction.

The visit was prolonged beyond all measure, because a zealous young manager explained in detail even things that required no explanation, with volleys of statistics that Comrade Petrovna had to translate without omitting a single one. Finally they came to the end of the assembly line. Don Camillo seemed to be thunderstruck with admiration at the sight of a finished tractor and said, turning to Peppone:

"Comrade Senator, this tractor is just like the one which the Soviet government presented to your agricultural cooperative at home!"

Peppone would gladly have committed mayhem. The tractor in question had stubbornly refused to work, and the whole province had laughed about it. Now he was forced to smile and say what a boon it was to his peasant constituents. But when he had finished his little speech the mechanic in him won the upper hand. He took aside one of the engineers and pointed out a certain part of the fuel injection pump, which he explained did not function for such and such a reason. The engineer listened attentively and then shrugged his shoulders since he could make no better reply. Fortunately Comrade Petrovna came over and offered to interpret for him.

"He gets the point," she said to Peppone. "They're waiting for authorization to make the necessary changes."

The engineer laughed and said something more, causing the girl to knit her brow and hesitate for a moment. Finally, without looking Peppone in the face, she added:

"He says the authorization may arrive from one year to the next."

She started to rejoin the group, but Scamoggia came to meet her.

"Comrade," he said, displaying a set of teeth as white as those of a Hollywood moving-picture idol, "I didn't hear those last figures about the replacement parts. Could you get the manager to repeat them?"

The manager obliged with a fresh volley of statistics, enough of them to choke an adding-machine. Scamoggia nodded approvingly and shook the manager's hand.

"Thank you," he said to Comrade Petrovna. "You don't know what pleasure you've given me."

"Are you particularly interested in agricultural machinery?" she inquired ingenuously.

"No, but I like to hear you talk."

This was a sacrilegious offense to a temple of labor and Comrade Petrovna paled and stiffened in proper bureaucratic style.

"Comrade . . ." she started to say in a harsh, metallic voice.

She had never been in the Trastevere section of Rome

or looked into a pair of eyes likes those of Scamoggia. They swallowed her up, and all her rigidity melted away.

R. was a typical Russian city of about a hundred and fifty thousand people, with few automobiles and little traffic of any kind on the streets. The hotel was small and ill-kept and Don Camillo found himself in a thoroughly uncomfortable room. He wondered with whom he was to share it, but his doubts were soon put to an end by the arrival of Peppone.

"Look here, Father—I mean Comrade—," said Peppone, "you've got to stop pulling Rondella's leg. Let him alone, even if you don't like him."

"But I do like him," Don Camillo said. "Where the Party's interests are at stake, I hew to the line. The fellow is sadly muddled; there are remnants of bourgeois ideology in his mind and it's up to us to clear them away."

Peppone threw his hat against the wall.

"One of these days I'm going to strangle you," he hissed into the priest's ear.

The group gathered in the dingy dining room. Comrade Oregov sat at the head of the table, with Peppone on his right and Comrade Nadia at his left. Don Camillo maneuvered himself into a place opposite Rondella, thus causing Peppone's temperature to boil over. It boiled over again when he saw Don Camillo raise his hand to his forehead to make the sign of the cross as he sat down.

"Comrades," he exploded, "what wouldn't I give if some of those stupid reactionaries who are always talking down the Soviet Union could be with us? If only they could see it with their own eyes!"

"It wouldn't be any use, Comrade," Don Camillo said dismally. What with pretending to smooth his hair and brush the lapels of his jacket, he had successfully made his sign of the cross. "Their own eyes wouldn't convince them. They go around with blinders."

Comrade Petrovna translated these words, and the tourist-bureau official nodded his shaven head in approval as he murmured a reply.

"Comrade Oregov says that you have hit the nail on the head," she said to Don Camillo, who acknowledged the compliment with a slight bow.

Scamoggia, who was always ready to second what Comrade Tarocci said, added an observation of his own.

"Our country is a century behind. Our stinking industrialists think they know it all, just because they produce a few miserable machines. But if they were to see a factory like the one we visited today, they'd have heart failure. And it isn't one of your biggest and best, is it, Comrade Petrovna?"

"Oh no, it's just a second-rate plant," she responded. "It's the last word in modern technology, but the production is relatively small."

Don Camillo shook his head sadly.

"We Italians ought to feel humiliated to see that a second-rate Soviet factory is so far ahead of the Fiat Company, which is our greatest producer of cars."

Comrade Peratto, from Turin, who so far had had very little to say, was wounded in his local pride.

"That may go for the tractor department, but when it comes to cars, the Fiat's not to be sneezed at. We have no right to belittle the Italian workers who made it what it is today."

"Truth above everything!" exclaimed Don Camillo. "Truth is more important than the pride of the Fiat Company. As long as national pride leads us to condone the backwardness of our social and economic system we shall never learn the lesson of efficiency which the Soviet Union can teach us. A man whose fiancée had only one leg insisted that two-legged women were inferior to her. That's exactly the attitude we have toward our half-baked accomplishments. Here in Russia industry has two strong legs to stand on."

"And what legs!" echoed Scamoggia, looking boldly at Comrade Petrovna.

"I don't see what you're driving at," Comrade Rondella said to Don Camillo.

"A Communist must face up to the truth, even when it is painful," Don Camillo explained. "We've come here to search for the truth, not to indulge in sentimentality."

The tourist-bureau official had followed the conversation carefully, asking Comrade Petrovna to translate every word. Peppone was sitting nervously on the edge of his chair, but fortunately just at this moment the food was brought to the table and the hungry group fell eagerly upon it.

The cabbage soup was not to their liking, but its taste was eclipsed by a savory roast of mutton. Their hosts had even thought to provide them with wine, which relaxed the tension and loosened their tongues. The subject of the tractor factory was brought up again and Comrade Peratto, in order to wipe out the bad impression he had made by boasting of Fiat cars, called Don Camillo's attention to the ingenuity of a certain device in the Russian tractor factory's assembly line.

"Of course," said Don Camillo; "the Russian people are ingenious and inventive above all others. They have demonstrated their talent not only in the invention of the radio and the sputnik but also in the perfection of all sorts of lesser gadgets. Take the washbasins in our bedrooms, for instance. Instead of having one tap for hot water and another for cold, they join them together in a single outlet which allows you to run water of whatever temperature you choose. This may seem like a small thing, but where else are you to find it?"

Rondella happened to be a plumber and he could not let this go by.

"Comrade, don't be silly. My grandfather knew how to put two taps together. Where do you come from?"

"From the part of Italy that has more Communists than any other; in other words, from the most progressive part of the country. Besides, if I'm silly, I'm in good company. In Churchill's memoirs you can find the very same thing, and nobody can say that Churchill's a Communist."

Rondella's ideas were not muddled; they were crystal clear and he insisted upon expressing them.

"I don't give a damn about Churchill! I say that by exaggerating these things you play right into the enemy's hands. If truth comes above everything, then we must show it some respect."

Don Camillo took off his misted glasses, wiped them and put them back on his nose. Then he broke the silence with these solemn words:

"Truth? Truth is whatever coincides with the interests of the working class. Comrades, you trust your eyes rather than your reason. And your reason is weak, because there are too many capitalistic cobwebs in your brain."

"And you have a brain like a sieve," Rondella retorted angrily. "Besides that, you've gone out of your way to step on my toes ever since we met. When we get back home, I'll take care of you!"

"I'm not as patient as you are," said Don Camillo, "and I'll take care of you here and now!"

It all happened in a flash. Rondella stood up and punched Don Camillo in the jaw and Don Camillo shot him a return blow which toppled him back into his seat. The tourist bureau official conferred with the interpreter and she passed on what he had to say to Peppone. Peppone got up, took Rondella by the scruff of his neck and hustled him outside.

"Comrade," he said when Rondella had recovered some

degree of composure, "the commissar noticed that you were out of sorts. Apparently this climate doesn't agree with you. An hour from now an airplane leaves for Berlin, and he can arrange for your finding a place on it. From there you can go straight home."

"With pleasure!" shouted Rondella. "You can't imagine how glad I'll be to see the last of the whole bunch of you."

"Don't take it so hard. We'll see you when we return."

Rondella opened his wallet, took out his Party membership card and tore it to pieces.

"We may meet," he said, "but I'll be on the other side of the street."

Peppone had to give him a kick in the pants, but he did so with sincere regret. When he came back into the dining room he put on a brave smile.

"It's all settled. He's most grateful for Comrade Oregov's thoughtfulness."

Then he raised his glass and proposed a toast to the victorious Soviet Union, to which Comrade Oregov responded with a toast to peace and the forthcoming liberation of the Italian working class from capitalist tyranny.

"How about drinking to Nadia?" Scamoggia whispered in Don Camillo's ear.

"Take it easy, Comrade!" was Don Camillo's reply.

The dinner ended on a gay note. An hour later, while Comrade Rondella was flying toward Berlin, with a befuddled head and an aching behind, Peppone and Don Camillo retired to their room.

"Put out the light, Comrade," said Don Camillo. "You can put it on again as soon as we're in bed."

"Ridiculous!" exclaimed Peppone.

"Ridiculous, my eye! A priest can't be seen in his underwear by a Communist senator!"

When the light went back on Don Camillo took a notebook and wrote in it: *"Return to the fold of Comrade Walter Rondella."* Out loud he said:

"Another redskin bites the dust!"

"Only a priest could play so filthy a trick! But you're not putting over anything else on me!"

Don Camillo sighed.

"You'll have to consult the inhabitant of my pen about that."

Peppone stared at it with fascination, while Don Camillo unscrewed the top and extracted a slender object which turned out to be a crucifix.

"Lord," said Don Camillo, raising his eyes to heaven, "forgive me for putting hinges on Your arms and on those of the Cross. But there was no other way I could bring You with me."

"Amen!" roared Peppone, burying his head under the sheet.

5

A Forced Rest

*"In illo tempore: Missus est Angelus Gabriel a
Deo in civitatem Galilaeae cui nomen Nazareth,
ad Virginem desponsatam viro, cui nomen erat
Joseph, de domo David, et nomen Virginis Maria.
Et ingressus Angelus ad eam dixit: Ave gratia
plena; Dominus tecum. . . ."*

The airplane on which he was traveling, together with
the druggist, swooped so abruptly that Peppone was left
gasping. He wondered confusedly what the Latin was
doing way up there in the air and how that hatefully
reactionary druggist had come to be with him on the trip
to Russia. Before he could settle these questions in his
mind the droning Latin broke in on his consciousness again.

*"Quae cum audisset, turbata est in sermone
eius, et cogitabat qualis esset ista salutatio. At ait
Angelus ei: Ne timeas Maria, invenisti enim
gratiam apud Deum. . . ."*

With enormous difficulty Peppone raised an eyelid which
seemed to weigh half a ton. Gradually his eye fell upon a
faded tapestry hanging on the wall with Russian characters
inscribed on it.

". . . *et vocabis nomen eius Jesum. Hic erit
magnus, et Filius Altissimi vocabitur.* . . ."

Peppone opened his other eye and turned completely
over. He was aghast to see that at the table which the
Soviet hotel administration had allotted to this room Comrade Camillo Tarocci was celebrating Mass. Out of the red-
jacketed volume of excerpts from Lenin he was reading
the Gospel according to St. Luke.

Peppone leaped out of bed and ran to hold his eye to
the keyhole of the door. His heart was pounding and for
a moment he thought the only thing to do was to throw a
sheet over Don Camillo's head. He thought better of this
and began to shuffle around the room, making as much
noise as possible in order to cover up the Latin sounds.
He would have continued this indefinitely, had not the
tinkle of a damned little bell rung in his buzzing ears. He
didn't want to listen, but he was forced to acknowledge its
reality, and when Don Camillo raised the tin cup which was
serving as a chalice, he came to a halt and bowed his head.
Steps rang out in the corridor, but Peppone did not budge.

"God help us!" he muttered to himself.

The steps stopped in front of the door; someone knocked
and said in almost unrecognizable Italian:

"Time to get up, Comrade!"

Peppone grunted an answer, and the steps moved on to
the next door.

"*Ite, Missa est.* . . ." said Don Camillo at last.

"It's about time," gasped Peppone. "You can keep the
blessing for yourself."

"Lord, forgive him," whispered Don Camillo, bowing
before the tiny crucifix which he had set up on the up-
turned bottom of an empty water carafe. "He's so jittery
he can't think straight."

"I'd like to know if you weren't jittery when they
knocked at the door," roared Peppone.

"Did somebody knock? I didn't hear."

Peppone didn't press the point because he knew that Don Camillo was telling the truth. Besides, he was dead tired and only wished he could go back to bed, even if it meant resuming his dream trip with the reactionary druggist.

"You're all ready, and the least you can do is get your trappings out of the way so that I can have room to dress," he said roughly.

"Comrade, you seem to be upset," said Don Camillo with a deadpan face. "Perhaps the climate of the Soviet Union doesn't agree with you."

"You're what upsets me!" shouted Peppone, shoving him through the door.

Then he saw something that upset him still more. The door wasn't locked, and whoever had come to call them could have simply turned the handle and walked in.

Comrade Nadia Petrovna was waiting at the breakfast table. As soon as they were all gathered together she said:

"We may as well start. Comrade Oregov won't be down for some time."

She was wearing her most forbiddingly bureaucratic manner and she spoke in a cold, impersonal voice, without looking anyone in the eye. Without a single unnecessary movement she lowered herself into a chair. She breakfasted on just a cup of tea, which she sipped distractedly, as if it were an unpleasant duty. It seemed as if she were enveloped in a sheath of ice, but, fortunately or unfortunately, there were cracks in the sheath and from them there issued an agreeable fragrance, which spoiled the effect of frigidity. Forgetful of the fact that she was a servant of the State, Nadia Petrovna had sprayed herself with the eau-de-cologne given to her by Comrade Nanni Scamoggia. Comrade Scamoggia was sitting at some distance from her, but he had a keen sense of smell and was quite aware of the transformation.

Comrade Yenka Oregov arrived just as breakfast was over. He had a preoccupied air, and after a hasty good morning he took Comrade Petrovna aside. They held a long discussion, making frequent reference to a piece of officially stamped paper which Comrade Oregov had taken out of his brief case. After they had apparently established a course of procedure, Comrade Petrovna addressed herself to Peppone.

"Comrade Yenka Oregov has received from the tourist bureau a definite program for the whole period of your stay. At nine o'clock this morning you are to visit the Red Star tractor factory."

Peppone stared at her in amazement.

"Comrade, if I'm not mistaken, that is the factory we visited yesterday afternoon."

Comrade Petrovna went back to confer with Comrade Oregov.

"The program which we have just received states unequivocally that after resting from your trip yesterday afternoon, you are to visit the factory today. The original program has been canceled and therefore yesterday's visit must be considered as not having taken place."

Peppone threw out his arms in bewilderment and she conferred again with her superior.

"The program is not subject to change, and this afternoon you are scheduled to take a sight-seeing trip around the city. Comrade Oregov does not insist that you pay another visit to the factory and so he suggests that you dedicate this morning to further rest, here in the hotel."

The travelers had not yet fully recovered from the weariness of their journey and so they jumped eagerly at this solution.

"Comrade Oregov is going to the factory to change the record of the date of your visit," said Comrade Petrovna. "I shall be at your service in the lobby."

And she went to sit on a broken-down sofa in the room

through which it was necessary to pass going either in or out of the hotel. Her bearing was stiff and proud, but she left a train of fragrant eau-de-cologne behind her.

Don Camillo went back up to his room, took off his shoes and threw himself down on his bed. But just as he was about to doze off, Peppone began to mutter to himself and pace the floor. After making his ablutions on the plane he had left his safety razor behind him.

"Take my razor and stop making such a racket," said Don Camillo.

"I never use any razor but my own," said Peppone. "And besides, I'm not used to that old-fashioned straight kind."

"Then go downstairs, change some of the liras you've taken from the taxpayers into rubles and buy yourself a new one. The General Store is nearby. Only be careful of the traffic and don't get yourself run over."

From the window there was not a car to be seen except for the bus which had brought them to the hotel, and Peppone was needled.

"The traffic will come in due time," he snorted. "We're not in a hurry. We are satisfied for the moment with the traffic with which we've peopled outer space."

"Buy me some wool socks," Don Camillo shouted after him. "In the forty years since the Revolution they must have made at least one pair."

Peppone slammed the door in reply.

Comrade Petrovna treated him with the utmost consideration and got the hotel manager to exchange his bank note for a package of rubles. Then she wrote in Russian on a slip of paper: *One safety razor and a dozen blades; one pair of men's wool socks, medium size.*

The General Store was just across the street and the transaction was speedily effected. As soon as the salesgirl had read the request she handed the items to Peppone and wrote down the price. But when Peppone returned to

his hotel room he did not look as happy as might have
been expected. He tossed the socks to Don Camillo, who
caught them in mid-air and looked at them with evident
satisfaction.

"Beauties!" he exclaimed. "We couldn't make anything
half so good. The idea of having one longer than another
is particularly clever. No man's feet are exactly the same.
How much did they cost?"

"Ten rubles," said Peppone, who was unwrapping his
razor.

"And what was the exchange?"

"I don't know. All I can tell you is that for a ten-thousand-lira bill they gave me seventy rubles."

"Then they gave you a hundred and fifty lira to a
ruble. It's just about the same as the Swiss franc. What
did you pay for the razor?"

"Nine rubles."

Don Camillo made some mental calculations.

"The razor was one thousand three hundred liras and
the socks one thousand four hundred and fifty."

Peppone was busily lathering his face and did not reply.

"How much would you pay for a razor like this at
home?" Don Camillo insisted.

"Two hundred liras for an American brand," admitted
Peppone. "I can't believe there's such a difference. It
must be a mistake."

"I don't think so, Comrade. You probably got your old
razor at a sale and you can't expect them to have such
things here. Under the Communist regime both factories
and retail shops belong to the State and they don't have
to meet any competition. Besides your razor was American
and this one is Russian; obviously there's no comparison
between them. Then although the ruble's worth only forty
liras on the free market, the tourist rate is a hundred
and fifty. Communism hasn't been fighting its way for

forty years just to give favorable exchange to visitors from abroad. Your razor would cost a Russian only three hundred and fifty liras."

Peppone had begun to shave. Suddenly he stopped, lathered his face again, changed the blade and started all over. Don Camillo stared at him quite pitilessly, but Peppone went grimly ahead. Then all of a sudden he swore and threw the razor at the wall.

"Comrade, where's your faith?" said Don Camillo gravely.

Peppone, his face still covered with lather, shot him a bitter glance. Don Camillo relented; he searched his own suitcase and found an object which he handed over to Peppone.

"Is this that disgusting American razor of yours?" he asked. "I found it on the floor."

Peppone snatched it from him.

"Every day I live I'm more sure that to murder a priest is no crime!"

Meanwhile, as Comrade Petrovna kept watch at the front door, Comrade Scamoggia appeared before her. Before he could open his mouth she said brusquely:

"Comrade Oregov asked you to dedicate this morning to resting up in the hotel. It's not right for you to try to go out."

"I'm not trying to go out," said Scamoggia. "I want to rest up here beside you."

Comrade Petrovna gave him a puzzled stare.

"With so much room in the hotel I can't understand why you choose to rest in this particular spot."

"Must you treat your comrades so very formally?"

"No, only capitalists go in for formality."

"But I'm not a capitalist!" Scamoggia protested.

"You have certain capitalist ways."

"I may have made a mistake, Comrade. If you're willing to help me I'll conduct a self-examination."

Comrade Petrovna was softened by the earnestness of these words.

"Sit down, Comrade," she said, without altogether abandoning her severity. "Tell me about yourself."

"My name is Nanni Scamoggia. I'm twenty-eight years old and I've been a member of the Communist Party ever since I attained the age of reason. I sell and repair scooters."

"What are scooters?"

He pulled out of his pocket a photograph of himself, a muscular figure in white overalls astride a Vespa.

"There you are," he said. "Practically everybody has one."

"Very interesting. And do the other members of your family belong to the Party?"

"My father's a member of the Leghorn section. My mother's dead. My sister is a cell leader in the Dressmakers' Union."

"And your wife?"

"Comrade, do I look like a married man?"

She stared at him severely.

"At your age you need a woman."

"But why should I tie myself down to one woman, when there are so many available?"

Instinctively she drew away.

"There's another instance of bourgeois mentality. Only capitalists exploit women by treating them like playthings. In a socialist society a woman has the same station and dignity as a man."

"Comrade, I didn't express myself correctly. I was speaking of that category of women who hate work and have no political or social principles. They have no dignity and therefore no rights. . . ."

"I understand," she interrupted. "But when a comrade

reaches a certain age, he ought to have a family and raise up new members of the Party."

"Comrade, I agree. But we live in a world very different from yours, full of selfishness and hypocrisy. In our country priests have the upper hand and a large number of women are obedient to them. Many of them are secret agents of the clergy, and a man has to watch his step."

"Don't you know any good Communist girls?"

"Yes, quite a few," he said with a weary gesture. "Perhaps it's all my fault, but I don't really care for any one of them."

"I can't believe it, Comrade. Not a single one?"

"Oh, one or two, perhaps. But they're already married."

Comrade Petrovna thought for a moment and then said:

"It's a serious situation, Comrade, I can see. But you're not facing up to it the way you should."

"Comrade," said Scamoggia, letting down his defenses, "the years go by, I know but with our blue sky and bright sun, all the flowers growing around us, the music in the air and the good wine we have to drink, a man has the illusion of being forever young. Our country has been blessed by God. . . ."

"*Comrade!*" she interrupted. "That's heresy! No country is either blessed or cursed by God. God doesn't exist!"

"I know. Perhaps it's on account of those miserable priests, and all the churches and shrines . . . but somehow we have the illusion that He is really there."

"You're mentally confused, Comrade!"

"Perhaps you're right. But can't you look me in the eye when you tell me so?"

"I mustn't fall into the same error as Stalin," she thought to herself. "You can't expect Russians and Italians to speak the same language. Every country has its own climate and customs. A single key won't open every lock."

But Comrade Scamoggia broke in on her reflections.

"Let's talk about you," he suggested.

"I'm a Soviet woman," she answered proudly. "A Party member and an employee of the government tourist office. I'm twenty-six years old and I live in Moscow."

"Do you live alone?"

"No, unfortunately I don't," she answered, lowering her head. "I share my room with two other girls. But I have no reason to complain."

"I'm not complaining either!" exclaimed Scamoggia.

Comrade Petrovna raised her eyes and looked at him with surprise.

"What do you mean?"

"I thought you might live with a masculine comrade. Naturally I'm glad to hear you live with two other girls."

She continued to stare at him.

"I don't follow your reasoning," she said.

But this was a shameless lie. It was quite clear from the fact that she turned his photograph over and over in her hands and instead of giving it back to him slipped it into her bag. Even a dyed-in-the-wool Communist bureaucrat is subject to human frailty.

6
The Space Cell

Except for Don Camillo, every member of the carefully chosen group was a Party militant of long standing —even the ill-fated Rondella, whom Don Camillo had perfidiously broken down and eliminated. Of the eight remaining stalwarts, Comrade Bacciga was perhaps the most solidly grounded in Communist doctrine, which he quoted at length on all appropriate occasions.

But Bacciga came from Genoa, and he was Genoese to the bone. Which means that he was above all a practical man, with a highly developed sense of business. Once Don Camillo had picked him for his next target this very sense of business was his undoing.

It happened on the afternoon of the first officially scheduled day, when the visitors were escorted on a sight-seeing tour of the city. The government-managed General Store, which Peppone had visited in the morning, was the first stop. Comrade Yenka Oregov instructed Comrade Nadia Petrovna to inform the visitors that by 1965 the Soviet Union would be producing eight billion yards of woolen materials a year and five hundred and fifteen million pairs of socks. Then, having assured them that everyone was free to buy what he chose, he stationed himself at the door to assure order.

Comrade Scamoggia wanted to know every detail of the store's operations and managed to draw Comrade

Petrovna aside, into the housewares department. Peppone attached himself like a watchdog to Don Camillo and the others scattered in different directions.

The store was full of women, many of whom wore a worker's smock or the uniform of a mail-carrier or a trolley conductor. After making some purchases of food or household goods they went, for the most part, to admire the displays of women's dresses, shoes, underwear and beauty products.

"*Your true Communist woman,*" Don Camillo said to Peppone, "*is remarkable for her lack of vanity and her scorn for everything superfluous.* On this premise there are only two possible explanations of the sight we have before us. Either these women are not good Communists, or else, thanks to the high living standards attained by the Soviet Union, the things they are gaping at with such obvious envy are not to be considered superfluous."

"I don't see what you're driving at," muttered Peppone suspiciously.

"I mean that consumer goods are now so abundant that a woman may allow herself to feel like exchanging her trousers for a pretty dress."

And when Peppone did not rise to this bait, he continued:

"After all the rubles you got for your ten thousand liras, why don't you buy a petticoat for your wife? Of course, a State petticoat, made out of State material by State dressmakers, can't be expected to have the trimmings and fine points of a privately manufactured product."

At this point Peppone could no longer withhold a withering reply.

"It's better for a woman to wear a plain petticoat and to be free, than to shop at Christian Dior's and be a slave."

"Well spoken, Comrade," said Don Camillo, who meanwhile had caught sight of the member of the group he was looking for.

Comrade Bacciga had managed to get away from the others and to engage in conversation with the clerk in the fur department. Their conversation was in sign language and in quotations of bid and asked, which they jotted down in turn on slips of paper. After they had come to an agreement Comrade Bacciga pulled some shiny cellophane envelopes out of his pocket which she nimbly stowed under the counter. Then she wrapped up a mink stole for him to take away and the transaction was completed. Peppone had not noticed what was going on, but Don Camillo had followed every stage of the proceedings and now he was in a hurry to return to the hotel.

But they did not return until evening, for after the General Store they visited a hospital and a ball-bearing factory. Don Camillo went straight to his room, and Peppone, worried by his disappearance, hastened to rejoin him. He found Don Camillo sitting on the floor, studying some pamphlets and papers he had taken out of his suitcase.

"Couldn't you be satisfied with the excerpts from Lenin?" roared Peppone. "What other rubbish did you bring with you?"

Don Camillo did not so much as raise his head, but continued his scrutiny.

"Take this," he said to Peppone, handing him a loose page, "and learn by heart the passages underlined with a blue pencil."

Peppone took one look at the page and started.

"This is something from the *Militant's Manual!*" he exclaimed.

"Well, what of it? Did you expect me to bring clippings from the *Osservatore Romano?*"

Peppone turned as violently red as the October Revolution.

"I say that this has been taken out of my own personal copy which belongs on the shelves of the local Party library!" he protested. "There's the library mark in it, right there. I'd like to know how. . . ."

"Don't be excited, Comrade. You don't suppose I could have acquired my Communist culture in the library of the Archbishop's Palace, do you?"

Peppone leaned over to examine the material on the floor.

"Every bit of it's mine!" he exclaimed in horror. "You've ruined the whole collection! I'll. . . ."

"Come now, Comrade!" interrupted Don Camillo. "It's disgraceful to rake up our petty personal differences here in a foreign land. Hurry up and memorize the passages underlined in blue. Those underlined in red are for me."

Peppone stared at him suspiciously.

"You're cooking up some mischief, for sure."

"Nothing of the sort. If you don't want to play the fool, go ahead and learn what I told you. You've got only half an hour."

"Very well. I'll have more to say to you later."

He sat down at the table, fixed his attention on the text and proceeded to learn his lesson. There were only two passages of a few lines each, but he was so indignant that he could have memorized a whole page.

"Now, let's hear you," said Don Camillo, putting the other papers back in the suitcase.

"Comrades!" said Peppone, "Lenin has said: '*Extremes are never advisable. But if we have to choose, we prefer absolute clarity, even if it is narrow and intolerant, to elusive and intangible haziness. . . .*'"

"Good! When I pretend that I can't remember a certain quotation from Lenin, then you are to come out with that. As for the other passage, your cue is when I ask you for the official opinion of the Party."

"For God's sake, what Party do you mean?"

"The one and only Communist Party, of course," said
Don Camillo. "Which, as it says in the *Manual, 'demands
of all its members that they. . . .'*"

"*. . . that they should, in their personal conduct. . . .*"
broke in Peppone. And angrily he recited the whole piece,
without omitting a single word or even a comma. Don
Camillo listened with a somewhat sanctimonious air and
said at the end:

"Good work, Comrade! I'm proud to be your pastor!"

Dinner was abundant and also educational, because
Comrade Oregov illustrated with numerous statistics the
progress which the Soviet Union would achieve in 1965.
At the end, after the customary toasts to peace, the easing
of international tension and the inevitable victory of Communism, Don Camillo rose from his chair.

"Comrades," he said, "Party membership obliges every
one of us to follow certain principles, to exercise self-
examination and constructive criticism of our fellows. . . ."

He talked very slowly, emphasizing every word and
looking proudly at Comrade Oregov, to whom Comrade
Petrovna conscientiously interpreted him.

"Before his Party conscience, a Communist must scru-
tinize his every action and question himself as to whether
he could have performed it better. He must not hesitate
to speak the truth, no matter how disagreeable it may be.
Comrade, I can't remember the exact words of Lenin on
this subject. Lenin said . . ."

He fumbled agonizingly for the words and Peppone put
in:

"Don't fret, Comrade. Lenin said: '*Extremes are never
advisable. But if we have to choose, we prefer absolute
clarity, even if it is narrow and intolerant, to elusive and
intangible haziness.*'"

Comrade Yenka Oregov nodded his head and smiled
complacently.

"Thank you, Comrade," said Don Camillo, keeping his eyes on Comrade Oregov. "On this basis I feel myself authorized to speak clearly. The little unpleasantness of yesterday, concerning Comrade Rondella, recalled to me the fifth paragraph of the Party Constitution, which says: '*In case of an infraction of Party discipline every member has a right to be judged by a regular Party organization and to appeal to the assembly of his fellow members and also to higher authorities.*' Now I have this to say: If one member of the group led by Comrade Senator Bottazzi is guilty of an infraction of Party discipline, what Party organization is to judge him? Of course the Comrade Senator represents the Party and can call his case to the attention of the federation, the regional section or the cell to which he belongs. But if the infraction is committed on Soviet soil and involves a local situation, who is to judge it? I maintain that it is to be judged here and now. Since we are not presently connected with any Party organization, such as those described in paragraph ten of the Party Constitution, I believe we can and should organize our own cell."

When Comrade Petrovna had translated these words, Comrade Oregov voiced no reaction and waited imperturbably for Don Camillo to go on.

"Comrades," he continued, "you look at me as if you were wondering what kind of cell I mean. Not a labor-union cell, since we are not engaged in labor; not a regional section, since this is not where we live. Of course it's true that we didn't come to the Soviet Union to amuse ourselves, but rather to learn and teach, and this is work of a very important kind. And even if we do not live here, the Soviet Union is our spiritual home. Let me tell you, then, what I have in mind."

Don Camillo was obviously sincere, and the others listened to him attentively.

"Comrades, we are a group of travelers who have removed themselves from an outworn, decrepit civilization and journeyed to a civilization which is in the pride of its youth. We are the crew of a flying machine which has left behind it the decaying world of capitalism and is making a voyage of exploration over the fascinating world of socialism. Our little crew is composed not of isolated individuals but of a group of men united by a single faith and a single will: to spread Communism throughout the globe. No, we are not a labor-union cell, or a regional section, we are an interplanetary cell, a space cell. For the world from which we came is more distant from the socialist world than this planet of ours from the moon. And so I propose that our group organize itself into a cell named for the one man who embodies the Soviet people's desire for peace and progress: Nikita Khrushchev!"

Comrade Oregov was so overcome with emotion that he stood up, amid ringing applause, and pumped Don Camillo's hand for at least ten minutes. Don Camillo conferred with him, through the interpreter, and then said:

"In the name of the Italian Communist Party and in agreement with the representative of the Communist Party of Russia, I announce the constitution of the 'Nikita Khrushchev Cell' "

The nine cell members held an immediate meeting, a very simple matter since they were all seated around the table, and pursuant to paragraph twenty-eight of the Constitution they voted for officers to represent them. Comrade Camillo Tarocci was elected leader; Comrade Nanni Scamoggia secretary and Comrade Vittorio Peratto treasurer. Peppone did not vote and it was not until he was raising his glass in a toast to the officers that he realized that the leader was to be Don Camillo. It was all he could do to choke down his glass of wine.

"Comrades," Don Camillo announced gravely, "I want first of all to thank you for this expression of confidence and to promise that I shall do everything I can to deserve it. I propose we start functioning without delay. Is there a suggestion of any business to be brought before the meeting?"

When no one spoke up, he jumped into the breach himself, to the accompaniment of an anguished glance from Peppone.

"Then, Comrades, I have something to suggest. No real Communist is afraid of the truth. The Party teaches us to be intolerant of failings, dissatisfied with anything that falls short of perfection. A Party member who is incapable of criticism, who does not demand a maximum of effort both of himself and his comrades cannot hope to be a leader or to win outsiders to the cause. Among the obligations listed in paragraph nine of the Constitution is that of 'leading a private life of exemplary integrity.' Comrade Bacciga, do you admit that this afternoon, in the course of our visit to the General Store, you bought a mink stole?"

"I do," replied Comrade Bacciga, turning deathly pale. "Comrade Oregov authorized us to buy anything we wanted."

"Correct. Do you further admit that you paid for the stole not with money but with nylon stockings which you brought from Italy? If you don't admit it, then you're a liar. And if you do, then you're admitting at the same time that you are party to one of those black-market transactions which are notoriously damaging to the Soviet economy, in short, that you're a saboteur. In either case your private life is not an example of integrity. With this I rest my accusation. Now the comrades will listen to your defense."

While Comrade Bacciga struggled to collect his thoughts Comrade Petrovna translated Don Camillo's words for the benefit of Comrade Oregov. When Comrade Bacciga did stammer a few lame excuses, they were unanimously judged to be insufficient. First, he had defrauded the

Soviet customs; second, he had sabotaged the Soviet economy; third, he had betrayed the trust of his Soviet comrades. Comrade Oregov looked like a Robespierre come to judgment, and Comrade Bacciga had to conduct his self-examination before him.

"The frank admission of your fault is in your favor," Don Camillo concluded. "But that is not enough. On this matter I shall ask the opinion of Comrade Senator Bottazzi."

Striking up as authoritative a pose as the circumstances would allow him, Peppone replied:

"The Party does indeed demand that every comrade's personal conduct should be an example to others. It cannot be indifferent toward behavior which lowers it in the public esteem. According to Marxist-Leninist philosophy, a Communist's private and Party life are one. The Party organization exercises a disciplinary function; it corrects such members as subordinate social responsibility to personal well-being and thereby tar themselves with the capitalist brush."

He delivered this harangue with such conviction that for the second time Comrade Oregov favored him with an approving smile.

"But self-examination and condemnation do not atone for a crime," Don Camillo added. "Even priests, who are the embodiment of hypocrisy and dishonor, tell a penitent that he must make amends for his sin, and in the case of theft he must return the stolen goods to their rightful owner."

"Comrade, you don't know priests!" Peppone interjected angrily. "They're much more likely to connive with the thief than to condemn him."

"I was speaking of what they *should* do rather than of their actual practice," Don Camillo explained. "Certainly Comrade Bacciga's barter must be considered a theft."

After some further talk Comrade Scamoggia entered a resolution:

"I move that the stolen object be restored to the Soviet Union. Let Comrade Bacciga give it to Comrade Nadia Petrovna."

There was a chorus of murmurs, interrupted by Comrade Petrovna in person.

"I am grateful for your kind thought," she said, "although it is to some extent 'tarred by the capitalist brush,' as the Comrade Senator was saying. But I have already told Comrade Oregov that you would like to give the stole to his wife, Comrade Sonia Oregovna."

This ingenious solution won a round of applause. Comrade Bacciga had to hand over the stolen stole to Peppone, who then presented it to Comrade Oregov, on behalf of the newly formed "Nikita Khrushchev Space Cell." As for the nylon stockings, they were entirely forgotten, that is except by Comrade Bacciga. When Don Camillo closed the meeting by sentencing Comrade Bacciga to six months of suspension from all Party activity, the latter shot him a look of fierce resentment. As they were going upstairs he caught up with his persecutor and hissed:

"Comrade, the Communist Party isn't big enough to hold the two of us!"

"Then surely the dishonest member should be the one to drop out," said Don Camillo.

Before putting out the light Don Camillo opened his famous notebook and wrote down: *"No. 2—Comrade Bacciga, morally liquidated."*

Peppone stretched his arm out of bed, snatched the notebook and read the annotation. Then tossing it back to Don Camillo he said:

"Your next entry will be: *'No. 3—Liquidated: The undersigned, by Comrade Peppone.'* "

Don Camillo looked down his nose.

"Comrade," he replied, "you forget that you're talking

to a leader. And a Communist leader isn't so easily liquidated."

"You don't know your Communist Party!" retorted Peppone.

7

Politics on the Road

"Comrade, have you the Party files of the members of our group with you?"

Peppone, who was busy shaving, wheeled angrily around.

"That's strictly my affair."

"Our affair, you mean. Now that I'm a cell leader I'm entitled to know my men."

"You're entitled to go straight to hell, and take your cell with you."

Don Camillo raised his eyes to heaven.

"Lord, did You hear him? Of all the Communist cells in the world this is the only one to have an accredited chaplain, and he says it can go to hell!"

Everything has its limits, and when a safety razor is used like a hoe it can be a very dangerous weapon. Peppone was hacking away at his chin, and his chin began to bleed. But how can a Communist senator have any peace of mind when he has brought with him to Russia a priest disguised as a Party militant of long standing and this diabolical Vatican emissary has set himself up as the leader of a cell? While Peppone was swabbing his nicked chin Don Camillo managed to replace in his roommate's suitcase the files which he had deftly taken out of it for study.

"Comrade, if those files are so very private," he said,

63

"let's forget about them. But don't be surprised if I make some embarrassing errors."

Just then Scamoggia came to tell them that the bus was waiting in front of the hotel.

It was a gray autumn morning. Women in men's coveralls were washing and sweeping the streets, running the trolley cars, tarring a paved square and doing construction work on a new building. In front of a *Gastronom* a long line of women, in simple but more feminine clothes, was patiently waiting. Don Camillo leaned toward Peppone and whispered in his ear:

"These women not only have men's rights; they have women's rights as well!"

Peppone did not even look up. He and Don Camillo were sitting on the back seats of the bus. Comrade Oregov and Comrade Petrovna sat in front, directly behind the driver, and the eight other comrades occupied the seats between. Whenever Comrade Petrovna stood up to translate some remark of Comrade Oregov she faced the entire group. This seating arrangement also allowed Don Camillo to talk in a low voice either to Peppone, who was sitting just across the aisle, or to Comrades Tavan and Scamoggia, who were sitting in the two seats directly ahead. Now that Don Camillo had liquidated Comrade Rondella of Milan and shaken the faith of Comrade Bacciga of Genoa, he was gunning for Comrade Tavan.

"Tavan, Antonio, forty-two years old, a native of Pranovo in the province of Veneto. Party member since 1943. Tenant farmer. Active, loyal, trustworthy. To be used only in peasant circles, on account of his limited acquaintance with social and economic problems. Socialist father. His family has worked the same land for 120 years. A skillful and hard-working farmer."

This was the description which Don Camillo had pilfered from Peppone's files, and now the peasant Tavan was a marked man.

They had left the city behind them and were traveling across the desolate countryside.

"We are now going through the 'Red Flag' *sovkos*," Comrade Petrovna was explaining, "one of the first of its kind to be established after the Revolution. It has a total area of 30,000 acres, of which 10,000 are under cultivation, and is equipped with fifty-four tractors, fifteen reaping machines and fifteen trucks. There are three hundred and eighty agricultural workers. At the present time there are six thousand *sovkos* in the Soviet Union, with a total of four million head of cattle, six million hogs and twelve million sheep. . . ."

Rising up out of the wide, flat land they suddenly saw signs of human habitation, small houses clustered around large buildings with corrugated iron roofs, silos, barns and warehouses As the bus bumped over a narrow dirt road, they noticed dozens of huge tractors abandoned hither and yon over the ploughed fields and covered with rust and mud. In the inhabited area other tractors, trucks and agricultural instruments stood about on the ground, exposed to the weather, in front of the farm buildings.

"Four million head of cattle!" exclaimed Don Camillo with a deep sigh.

"That's quite a number!" agreed Peppone.

"When you add those to the twenty-seven million of the *kolkhos*, they come to thirty-one million."

"Colossal!"

"By the end of 1960 there are supposed to be forty million," Don Camillo went on. "But for the time being there are still two million two hundred head less than there were in 1928, before collectivization."

Peppone could not see what Don Camillo was after.

"Comrade," Don Camillo explained, "the Soviet Union is the only country in the world where everything is out in the open, where there is a public statement of whether or not things are going well. These are official statistics and from them we must conclude that whereas there has been enormous progress in science and industry, agriculture is still lagging. Volunteers have had to be sent from Moscow, Kiev and other cities to break ground in Siberia."

He threw out his arms in mock sympathy, then aiming his words at the ears of the peasant Tavan he added, ostensibly to Peppone:

"Comrade, you've seen the condition of those tractors and you can judge for yourself the validity of my conclusions. I tell you that the trouble is this: peasants are peasants the world over. Just look at the way things are at home. Who are our most backward people? Peasants! Yes, I know that the day laborers are struggling to improve their situation, but they are workers. Just try to change the ways of a peasant or a tenant farmer! See if you can make him class-conscious or involve him in the proletarian movement!"

Comrade Tavan had pricked up his ears and was not losing a single word of the conversation going on behind him.

"And now consider the state of things here in Russia," continued Don Camillo. "What people are holding the country back? The hard-headed *kolkhos* holders, who don't give a hang for the collectivized land and insist upon cultivating the few acres which the government has generously given them for their own private use. There are eighty thousand *kolkhos* and six thousand *sovkos*, but the *kolkhos* peasants have seventeen million head of privately owned cattle, as compared to fourteen million collectively owned between *kolkhos* and *sovkos* together. Those peasants don't deserve to own any land at all. And, mark my words, it will be taken away from them."

Comrade Tavan's ears had turned bright red.

"Look again at our own country," said Don Camillo.

"Who promoted the black market during the war? The peasants! And who promotes it here? The peasants of the *kolkhos!* With us, where is it that the priests still have most power? Among the peasants! And in the Soviet Union how do the surviving priests continue to retard the general progress? Thanks to the rubles they collect from the *kolkhos!*"

Comrade Tavan's ears were no redder than the cheeks of Peppone.

"Comrade," said Don Camillo, by way of winding up his peroration, "here we have a country that has beaten world records in every domain and won first place in the race to the moon. But among the *kolkhos* you still find selfish obstruction to progress. Beware of peasants! They're an ugly lot, I tell you!"

"Well spoken, Comrade!" said Scamoggia, from his seat in front of Peppone. "People make me laugh when they talk about giving the peasants land. Give it to them, and see what they'll do! They'll starve us! The land should be publicly owned, cultivated by the State. And peasants should be treated like workers. Just because the peasants work the land, are they to have its produce? Then why shouldn't a worker in an automobile factory be given a car? Who gave us our Fascist regime? The peasants! Wasn't a black shirt their everyday working garment in Emilia and Romagna, where you and the Comrade Senator come from? . . . Just look at the way that stupid fool out there is assassinating that tractor! . . ."

The careening tractor in the immediate vicinity of the bus seemed dangerously out of control. As a matter of fact the driver was not a peasant; he was a government farm bureau agent. But although his ineptitude was not forwarding the sixth Five-year Plan it fitted in most opportunely with the purposes of Don Camillo.

"Lout!" called out Scamoggia as the tractor passed alarmingly close by.

But the lout took this interpellation for a friendly greeting and raised a clenched fist in reply. Comrade Tavan's ears had grown deadly pale. Peppone scribbled something on a scrap of paper and handed it to Don Camillo. For the benefit of their companions he said:

"Make a note on what we are seeing for the report we are to take back home."

But on the paper he had written:

"Keep your mouth shut, or I'll fracture your shin!"

Don Camillo nodded gravely. Meanwhile Scamoggia was distracted from his diatribe against the peasants by an explanatory harangue from Comrade Nadia Petrovna.

"We are not stopping at the 'Red Flag' *sovkos,* because it is concerned only with the cultivation of grain. The grain has already been harvested and there is nothing for us to see. We are proceeding now to the *kolkhos* at Grevinec, a cooperative enterprise covering four thousand acres of land, which goes in for truck gardening and for raising cattle and hogs as well. It is completely autonomous and receives no government aid, although the government farm bureau supplied its mechanical equipment. . . . Just now, Comrades, we have crossed the *kolkhos* boundary line. . . ."

This last bit of information was quite superfluous, because although the terrain was the same as before, the general picture was entirely different. Here everything was the way it should be; the fields were tidily ploughed and the grazing livestock well fed. The village houses were the usual wooden shacks, but each one had its own neatly trimmed orchard and vegetable garden, a chicken yard, a hog run and a stall for the cow. Two solidly constructed buildings housed the administrative offices and the community school. Comrade Petrovna explained that ninety-seven per cent of the *kolkhos* were electrified, but unfortunately this one belonged to the more primitive minority.

In order to reach the heart of the village the bus had

to go over a typically rutted road, and so while it was still half a mile away the "Space Cell" group requested permission to get out, stretch their legs and cover the remaining distance on foot. The mud had dried and hardened, and by taking care not to stumble into the ruts the visitors were able to walk without too much difficulty. Along the way they were overtaken by a horse and cart. In the cart sat a chubby man wearing high boots, an oilskin raincoat with a fur collar and a fur cap. Don Camillo scrutinized him attentively and hastened to catch up with Comrade Petrovna.

"Who is that fine gentleman, Comrade?" he asked her.

Comrade Petrovna laughed. She passed the question on to Comrade Oregov, who seemed to share her amusement.

"Comrade, you have eagle eyes," she said to Don Camillo. "That 'fine gentleman' is a priest."

"What? A priest?" exclaimed Comrade Scamoggia, who was of course walking at Comrade Petrovna's side. "What business has he here?"

She looked at him severely.

"Comrade, do you remember paragraph 128 of the Constitution: *'In order to assure freedom of conscience, the Church is separate from the State and the Schools from the Church. Every citizen has a right to observe religious practices or to conduct antireligious propaganda, as he chooses.'*"

"But that fellow's not a citizen, he's a priest!" said Scamoggia indignantly.

Comrade Petrovna laughed again and when she had explained the reason for her hilarity to Comrade Oregov he once more chimed in.

"Comrade," she said, "in the Soviet Union priests have the same rights as anyone else. As long as they do not go in for obnoxious proselytizing, no one disturbs them. If someone wants a priest, he is free to pay for his services."

Scamoggia turned to Don Camillo.

"Comrade, you were right. And to think that one of my reasons for wanting to come here was to get the priests out of my hair!"

"Priests are the lowest order of creatures on earth!" roared Peppone. "When Noah got into the ark, he didn't want to take any snakes along, but God Almighty shouted to him: 'Noah, without priests, how am I to survive?'"

When Comrade Oregov was informed of this witticism he laughed louder than ever and took it down in his note-book. Don Camillo laughed too, unenthusiastically, and fell back to the end of the line, where Peppone was walking.

"Comrade, that's cheating!" he protested. "I didn't tell you the story that way. Noah didn't want to take *donkeys*, and God said: 'Without Communist senators I wouldn't have any fun!'"

"My version is better," retorted Peppone. "Only I owe an apology to the snakes."

"You fraud!" hissed Don Camillo. "You're taking advantage of the fact that I'm a cell leader!"

They walked along in silence for a moment and then Peppone returned to the attack.

"I saw that fellow myself," he muttered; "all of us saw him. But you were the only one to detect the smell of a priest. The call of the blood, no doubt! But don't fool yourself. When we come to power you won't go about in a cart, or a car or even on your own two feet. Dead men don't stir."

"That's all right with me," said Don Camillo, calmly lighting the butt of his cigar. "Under a Communist regime anyone who stirs is dead, and one dead man's as good as another."

As they entered the village Scamoggia turned around and shouted back to Don Camillo:

"Comrade, you were right again when you said priests live off the ignorance of the peasants. Just look at that fellow now!"

In one of the vegetable gardens the priest was busily talking to an old couple. Don Camillo saw him plainly and so did Comrade Tavan. Once more the latter's flapping ears turned crimson. Comrade Petrovna shook her head.

"Don't get excited, Comrade," she said to Scamoggia. "He's in contact only with a few old people. That's the way it is all over. When they die off, then God will die, too. Even now He lives only in the minds of those who were brought up in an era of superstition. And when God is dead, the priests will follow. The Soviet Union has plenty of time ahead of it; we can afford to wait."

She spoke in a loud voice and even Don Camillo, at the end of the line, heard her.

"God can afford to wait too," he mumbled in the direction of the silent Peppone.

Comrade Salvatore Capece, a thirty-year-old Neapolitan, with an expressive face and flashing eyes, was standing nearby, and Don Camillo said to him provocatively:

"Comrade Petrovna has really got something, don't you agree?"

"She's got plenty," Capece eagerly responded. "I don't mind telling you that she's right up my alley."

Don Camillo smiled.

"From the way she keeps looking at you I think you've taken her fancy," he remarked.

Comrade Petrovna hadn't intentionally looked at him at all, but Capece was more than ready to swallow Don Camillo's flattery.

"Comrade, you know what's what," he agreed. "A woman can't be anything else but a woman."

And he quickened his step in order to rejoin her.

"You'll go to any lengths to stir up trouble, won't you?" said Peppone.

"Comrade, I've got to get busy while God is still alive. Tomorrow may be too late," said Don Camillo.

8

Christ's Secret Agent

GREVINEC WAS PREPARED for the Italian visitors' arrival; the propaganda and publicity director was waiting for them at the entrance to the village and led them to the administrative headquarters of the local soviet, where the district Party leader and the head of the *kolkhos* gave welcoming speeches, translated by Comrade Nadia Petrovna. Peppone made a carefully rehearsed speech in reply and followed the local custom of joining in the applause.

Besides the bigwigs there were several minor dignitaries whom Comrade Petrovna introduced as the directors of the various departments: cattle and hog breeding, fruit, vegetable and grain production, machinery repairs and so on. The room in which the reception was held was barnlike in structure, furnished with a rough wooden table, rows of chairs and a portrait of Lenin on the wall. The reception committee had adorned the gilt-framed portrait with green branches, but this decoration attracted less attention from the guests than did the presence of numerous bottles of vodka on the table.

A glass of vodka, downed as rapidly as if it were red wine, is stimulating to both heart and body, and Peppone responded promptly and intensely to it. After Comrade

Petrovna had explained that this particular *kolkhos* was a recognized champion in the production of pork, milk and cereals, he asked for the floor. Standing squarely in front of Comrade Oregov, he began to speak, quite extemporaneously, pausing after every sentence to give Comrade Petrovna time to translate it.

"Comrade," he said, "I come from the province of Emilia, where, exactly fifty years ago, some of the first and most successful people's cooperatives were established. In this region agriculture is highly mechanized, and the pork, dairy and cereal products are tops in quantity and quality alike. In my village my comrades and I have founded a cooperative of farm workers which was honored, not long ago, by a magnificent gift from the Soviet Union!"

Here Peppone pulled out of his brief case a sheaf of photographs, which he handed over to Comrade Oregov. The photographs showed the triumphant arrival in the village of "Nikita," the gift tractor, and its operation on the cooperative's land. They were passed around to all those present and received unanimous approval.

"In our country the undermining of capitalism is under way," Peppone continued. "It is not yet in the final stage, but it is making progress, as Comrade Tarocci, who comes from the same region, can testify. Inevitably the privileges of the landowners and clergy will be wiped out, and a new era of liberty will begin. Soon agricultural cooperatives modeled on the *kolkhos* and government projects modeled on the *sovkos* will replace the slave-labor conditions which form such a shameful hangover from the past. You can understand how deeply interested I am in the Russian *kolkhos*. I should like to ask Comrade Oregov and your leaders to show me every detail of the Grevinec operation."

Comrade Oregov replied that he did indeed understand the importance of the Italian comrade's request and would do everything in his power to satisfy it. He parleyed with the *kolkhos* leaders, and Comrade Petrovna transmitted the gist of their deliberations to Peppone.

"Comrade, everyone appreciates your interest in the technical and organizational aspects of our undertaking. But if I were to act as an intermediary between you and the *kolkhos* leaders for the whole time of your visit, your comrades would not be able to make the complete tour of the area which the program provides for them. Fortunately, among the technicians here present there is one who can give you complete information in your own language."

She paused to beckon to one of the Russian group, and a thin, dark man between thirty-five and forty years old, in mechanic's garb, stepped forward.

"Here we have a man whose job is concerned with farm-machinery supplies and repairs, Stephan Bordonny, an Italian. . . ."

"Stephan Bordonny, citizen of the Soviet Union," the thin man interrupted, holding out his hand to Peppone, but looking reproachfully at Comrade Petrovna. "Yes, I am a Soviet citizen, and so are my children."

Comrade Petrovna smiled to cover up her embarrassment.

"I stand corrected, Citizen," she said. "I should have specified that you are of Italian origin. While the rest of us make a general tour, you will be a private guide to Comrade Senator Bottazzi."

She went to join the group and Don Camillo started to go after her, but Peppone blocked the way.

"You are to stay with me, Comrade Tarocci," he said firmly, "and to take notes on everything we see."

"At your orders, Comrade," said Don Camillo wryly.

"Are you a Party member, Comrade?" Peppone asked their guide.

"No, I haven't yet been accorded the honor," the other replied with an impersonal and detached air.

Citizen Bordonny gave definite answers, which Don Camillo transcribed in his notebook, to every question asked by Peppone, but it was plain that he did so in the least possible number of words. He knew every detail of the *kolkhos'* operation and cited exact dates and figures, but without any comment of his own. He courteously refused the cigar and the cigarette which Peppone and Don Camillo in turn offered him. Because they were smoking he finally took out of his pocket a piece of newspaper and a pinch of *makorka* and deftly rolled a cigarette. They visited the wheat silos and then the warehouse used to store fertilizers, sprays and small agricultural tools. Everything was listed and in perfect order.

In one corner of the warehouse was an odd-shaped, brand-new machine and Peppone asked what it was used for.

"It's for carding cotton," Bordonny replied.

"Cotton?" exclaimed Don Camillo. "Do you mean to tell me that in this climate you can grow cotton?"

"No," said Bordonny laconically.

"Then what are you doing with this machine?"

"It came here by mistake. We had asked for a threshing machine for our wheat."

Peppone shot Don Camillo an atomic glance, but Don Camillo had caught onto a good thing and had no intention of letting it go.

"So are you going to adapt it to threshing?" asked Don Camillo.

"No," their guide said icily. "We've put together a machine of our own."

"And how do you suppose the other fellows who ordered the carding machine are managing to handle their cotton?"

"That's not our affair."

"Mix-ups of this kind shouldn't be allowed," said Don Camillo with a curtness which equaled Bordonny's.

"The area of your country is a hundred and fifty thousand square miles, and ours is eleven million," answered the other.

At this point Peppone intervened, at the same time stepping with an utter lack of delicacy on Don Camillo's foot.

"Citizen Bordonny, are you in personal charge of this operation?" he inquired.

"No. I have only a limited share of the responsibility."

"I'd like to see some of the larger machines," said Peppone.

The warehouse for the larger machines was not much to look at. It was a big, wooden barn with a rusty corrugated-iron roof. But inside it was truly impressive. The beaten-earth floor was immaculately clean and the machines were polished and lined up as if for exhibit at a fair. Citizen Bordonny knew the date of purchase, the oil and gasoline consumption and the horsepower of every one.

At the far end of the building there was a workshop with brick walls. It contained a strict minimum of tools but it was kept in such perfect order that Peppone was very nearly moved to tears. A tractor was currently under repair and the various parts of its motor were lined up on a workbench. Peppone picked up one of the parts for closer examination.

"Who's been working on this?" he asked.

"I have," said Citizen Bordonny indifferently.

"With this lathe?" asked Peppone, pointing in surprise to an instrument that had nothing vaguely lathe-like about it.

"No, with a file," the guide answered.

Hanging from a big hook on the wall there was a connecting rod, tied together with heavy string. Bordonny took a screwdriver and struck the rod, causing it to ring like a bell.

"It's out of balance," he said. "I can tell from the sound. All it takes is a practiced ear."

Peppone took off his hat and wiped the perspiration from his forehead.

"What do you know about that?" he exclaimed. "I thought there was only one man in the world who used that system. And here in the middle of Mother Russia I find another!"

"Who's that?" asked Don Camillo.

"The mechanic at Torricella," said Peppone. "A perfect wizard, who specialized in tuning racing-cars. A fellow that didn't look as if he had a penny to his name, but racers used to send him their cars from all over Europe. During the second year of the war his machine shop was hit by a bomb aimed at the bridge over the Stivone. He and his wife and two children were killed on the spot."

"Only one of his sons," said Bordonny. "The other was lucky enough to be in the army." There was a new tone in his voice as he added: "I'm happy to know someone who remembers my father."

They left the building in silence. Outside, the sky was black with an impending storm.

"I live in that house over there," said Bordonny. "We'd better take shelter there before it starts to pour. While we're waiting I can answer any further questions."

They reached the house just as the first drops of rain were beginning to fall. It was a simple dwelling, but cozy and warm, with smoke-blackened beams on the kitchen ceiling. Peppone had not yet recovered from his surprise when they sat down at the long table.

"The last time I went to your father's machine shop was in 1939," he said, as dreamily as if he were talking to himself. "Something was wrong with my little second-hand car and I couldn't get at the trouble."

"It was a connecting-rod," said Bordonny. "And I was

the one who fixed it. My father used me as a helper. Tell me, how did the car run?"

"It's still running. . . . So that slight boy with a lock of dark hair dangling over his forehead. . . ."

"I was just nineteen," said Bordonny. "And at that time you didn't have a mustache, as I remember."

"No," said Don Camillo. "He grew that when he was thrown in jail for drunkenness and disorderly conduct. Of course his real crime was anti-Fascist agitation, and eventually it did him a good turn. After the war he won the status of political prisoner and martyr to the cause. That's how he became first mayor and then senator."

Peppone brought down his fist on the table.

"That's not the whole story!" he protested.

Bordonny was staring at Don Camillo.

"Your face isn't unfamiliar either," he said. "Do you come from the same place?"

"No, no," Peppone hastily interpolated. "He's been living around there, but he comes from another town. You couldn't possibly have known him. Tell me, how did you get here?"

Bordonny shrugged his shoulders.

"What's the use of going back over things which the Russians have generously forgotten?" he said in a voice which had once more turned cold. "If you want more explanations about the *kolkhos*, I'm ready to give them to you."

But Don Camillo did not leave it at that.

"My friend, don't let the fact that he's a Communist senator stand in your way. We don't have to consider politics. You can talk as man to man."

Bordonny looked in the eyes of first the one and then the other.

"I have nothing to hide," he asserted. "Everybody here at Grevinec knows my story. But since they don't talk about it, I'd rather not talk about it either."

Don Camillo held out his pack of Italian cigarettes.

Outside there was a raging storm, and rain beat against the windowpanes.

"For seventeen years I've been craving one of those cigarettes," said Bordonny, lighting one up. "I've never got used to *makorka* rolled in newsprint. It makes my stomach turn over."

Greedily he inhaled a few puffs and then let the smoke trickle slowly out of his mouth.

"It's a simple story," he said. "I was on the Russian front, at a truck repair center, and one day the Russians walked in and took us over. It was the end of 1942, and the wind and snow were murderously cold. They drove us ahead of them like a flock of sheep. Every now and then one of us fell to the ground and they left him with a bullet in his head on the muddy snow. I fell, too, but I knew enough Russian to make myself understood and when a Russian soldier gave me a kick and said 'Get up!' I was able to answer. '*Tovarisch*,' I said, 'I can't go on. Let me die in peace.' I was one of the last prisoners in the column and the others were already a hundred feet away, almost lost from sight in the snow. He aimed above my head and muttered: 'Hurry up and die, then, and don't get me into trouble.' "

Just then somebody bundled up in dripping burlap came into the kitchen. Unwinding this covering she revealed herself to be a handsome woman no more than thirty years old.

"My wife," said Stephan.

The woman smiled, murmured a few incomprehensible words and disappeared up a circular stair.

"God willed that I should live," Bordonny went on. "When I came to I found myself in a warm *isba*. The place where I had fallen was half a mile from here, between the woods and the village, and a seventeen-year-old girl who had gone to collect kindling had heard moans coming out of a pile of snow. She had strong arms and she tugged me along on my coat collar, like a sack of potatoes, without even setting down her bundle of wood."

"They're good people, these Russian peasants," said Peppone. "A fellow called Bagò, from Moinetto, was saved in the same way."

"Yes, a lot of fellows owe them their lives. But this girl wasn't Russian; she was a Pole whose family had been moved here because there was a shortage of agricultural workers. They shared what little food they had with me and kept me hidden for two days. I realized this couldn't go on forever, and since the girl and I managed to communicate with each other in broken Russian, I told her to go report that a lost Italian soldier had stumbled in on them only a few hours before. Reluctantly she consented to go. Soon she came back with a man armed with a pistol and two others with guns. I raised my hands and they beckoned to me to follow them. The Polish family's hut was the one farthest from the center of the village, and I had to walk a good distance with the guns sticking into my back. Finally we came to the open space where you saw the silos. A truck loaded with bags of wheat was standing there and an unfortunate fellow was ruining the motor trying to get it started. I was so outraged that I turned to one of my captors and said: 'Tovarisch, he's going to run down the battery and then he'll never get it going at all. The injection pump must be choked; tell him to pump out the gasoline.' My guard was amazed to hear me use a few Russian words. 'What do you know about it?' he asked suspiciously. 'That's my trade,' I told him. The battery was rapidly dying, and he pushed me over to the truck and ordered the driver to do what I had said. The face that looked out of the cab window was that of a very young boy in soldier's uniform. He didn't know what pump I was talking about, because he'd never driven a diesel before. I asked for a screwdriver, threw up the hood and cleaned out the fuel injector. 'Now it will start,' I said, and a few minutes later he drove it away.

"They shut me up in a small room of the local soviet but left me a cigarette for company. Ten minutes later they came back, and holding their guns against my back, pushed me over to a shed where there were primitive arrangements to repair tractors and agricultural machinery. They pointed out one of the tractors and told me to find out what was the matter with it. I asked for some boiling water to pour into the radiator and then tried to start it. Then I got down and said: 'It's a cylinder. The whole motor has to be taken apart and the cylinder made over. It will take quite some time.' With the miserable tools they gave me I worked like mad for forty-eight hours. Just as I was putting back the whole block an officer and two men armed with submachineguns came along. They looked on while I put more boiling water in the radiator and tried the motor. God meant me to live, because it started right up and ran like a dream. I ran it around the shed and then brought it back to its original place. I wiped my hands on a rag, jumped down and stood in front of the officer with my arms above my head. They all started laughing. 'He's all yours, Comrade,' said the officer to the district Party leader. 'It's your responsibility; if he runs away, you'll pay for it.' I joined in the laughter. 'Captain,' I said, 'Russia's a big country, and I'm not likely to run any farther than that isolated *isba*, where there's a girl I've taken quite a fancy to, even if she did report me.' The officer looked me up and down. 'You're a good Italian worker,' he said. 'Why did you come to fight against the workers of the Soviet Union?' I told him that I came because I was sent. My only military activity was truck repairs and the only Russians I'd killed were two chickens I had accidentally run over. . . ."

The storm was raging more fiercely than ever. Bordonny

got up and talked into an old army field telephone in one corner. Then he came back and said:

"They say you may as well stay here. The rest of your party is stuck over at Barn No. 3, which is at the other end of nowhere." And he sat down.

"Well, what happened next?" asked Don Camillo.

"I worked like a dog at repairing their machines and putting the workshop in order. By the time I was able to stop and think the war was over. The Polish girl's father died, and we got married. As the years went by she and I were both given Soviet citizenship."

"And didn't you ever think of going home?" asked Don Camillo.

"What for? To see the mass of rubble where my father and brother were rotting away? Here they treat me as if I were one of their own, in fact better, because I'm good at my job. At home there's no one to remember me. I'm just one of the prisoners of war who disappeared in Russia. . . ."

Just then there was a loud noise and the door was thrown open. In came a stream of water and a strange wriggling monster that looked like a giant centipede. From somewhere Bordonny's wife appeared on the scene and rushed to close the door. The shiny oilskin covering of the monster fell to the floor and out popped half a dozen children, one handsomer than the next, ranging from six to twelve years of age.

"Your disappearance in Russia has been time well spent, I can see that!" exclaimed Don Camillo.

Bordonny stared at him again.

"I *do* have a feeling I've seen you before," he repeated.

"It's unlikely," said Don Camillo. "But even if you have, forget about it."

They were well-brought-up children and although for the first few minutes they made quite a racket, a few words from their mother were enough to calm them down. They sat down on a bench near the stove and began talking in a low voice together.

"They're still small," the woman apologized in surprisingly good Italian. "They forgot that their grandmother is sick in bed upstairs."

"May we pay her a visit?" said Don Camillo.

"That would make her very happy. She seldom has a chance to see anybody."

They went up the circular stair to a low-ceilinged attic room. A shriveled old woman was lying in a bed made up with neatly pressed white sheets. Bordonny's wife said something to her in Polish and she whispered a reply.

"She says may the Lord bless those who visit the sick," the wife explained. "She's very old and she can't help thinking in terms of the past."

At the head of the bed there was a holy picture and Don Camillo bent over to examine it.

"It's the Black Madonna!" he exclaimed.

"Yes," murmured the wife, "the protectress of Poland. Old Poles are Catholics. On account of her age you must forgive her."

She spoke cautiously and there was a vague look of fear in her eyes.

Peppone put in a reassuring word.

"There's nothing to forgive. In Italy young people are Catholics, too. It's quite all right as long as they're on the level. Our enemies are the priests, because they mix politics with religion."

The old woman whispered something into her daughter's ear and the latter shot an enquiring glance at Bordonny.

"They're not here to do us any harm," he told her.

"Mother wants to hear how is . . . the Pope," his wife stammered.

"He's all too healthy!" answered Peppone.

Don Camillo extracted something from an inside pocket.

The old woman stared at it with wide-open eyes and then reached out a bony hand. She whispered excitedly into her daughter's ear.

"She wants to know if that's really he."

"Himself and no other. Pope JOHN XXIII."

Peppone turned pale and looked around him with a worried air.

"Comrade," said Don Camillo, taking him by the arm and impelling him toward the door, "go downstairs with Citizen Bordonny and see if it's still raining."

Peppone started to protest, but Don Camillo cut him short.

"Don't interfere with me, Comrade, if you value your skin."

And he stayed alone with the two women.

"Tell your mother she can talk freely, because I'm as much of a Catholic as she is."

The two women spoke at length together and then the younger one reported:

"She wants to thank you and give you her blessing. Now that she has that picture she feels that she can die in peace. It was very hard for her to see my father die without the last rites of the Church."

"But there are priests of a sort, who are free to visit you, aren't there?" asked Don Camillo.

She shook her head.

"They seem like priests," she explained, "but they are emissaries not of God but of the Party. What good are they to us Poles?"

The rain was still coming down in buckets. Don Camillo took off his jacket, pulled the hinged crucifix out of the false fountain pen, stuck it into the neck of a bottle and set it upon the bedside table. Then he took out the aluminum cup which served for a chalice.

A quarter of an hour later, Peppone and Bordonny,

alarmed by the long silence, came upstairs and looked in the door. Before their startled eyes Don Camillo was celebrating Mass and the old woman, her hands folded and her eyes filled with tears, was following his every motion. After she had received communion it seemed as if new strength were flowing through her veins.

"*Ite, missa est. . . .*"

The old woman whispered breathlessly into her daughter's ear and the latter went to stand beside her husband.

"Father," she said excitedly, "will you marry us before God? Until now we've been married only in the sight of man."

Outside the rain was still coming down as hard as if clouds from all Russia had converged upon Grevinec. There was no wedding ring, but the old woman slipped a worn gold band off her fourth finger.

"Lord," said Don Camillo, "don't take it amiss if I skip a few words or even a few sentences. . . ."

Peppone stood there like a stone until Don Camillo pushed him down the stairs.

"Go bring them up here, the whole lot of them!" he ordered.

The rain had begun to diminish, but Don Camillo was so wound up that he could not stop. In the twinkling of an eye he baptized all the children. And yet he did not, as he had threatened, skip a single word, much less a sentence. Only God could have given him the wind to get through it.

The whole thing lasted an hour, or perhaps it was a minute. Before he knew it Don Camillo was sitting once more at the kitchen table, with Peppone at his side and Bordonny across from him. The sun had come out and the children's eyes were shining in the dark corner. Don Camillo counted them: twelve for the children, four for their parents and two for the old woman. She was not with them downstairs, but her eyes were indelibly imprinted on his memory, for he had never seen a look such as theirs before.

Just then Comrade Nadia Petrovna appeared at the door.

"Is everything all right?" she inquired.

"Everything's perfect," said Don Camillo.

"We are most grateful to Comrade Oregov for assigning us a guide as competent as Citizen Stephan Bordonny," added Peppone, shaking their host's hand and starting toward the door. Don Camillo was the last to leave the house, and at the threshold he turned around to make the sign of the cross.

"*Pax vobiscum*," he murmured.

And the old woman's eyes responded:

"*Amen.*"

9

The Rains Came to Stay

As it was categorically stated on the visitors' program, they were guests of the Grevinec *kolkhos* for lunch, and this spontaneous generosity aroused the expected enthusiasm among them. Peppone had prudently arranged for Don Camillo to sit beside him, and now Don Camillo whispered in his ear:

"Comrade, I have no use for people who find everything abroad superior to what they have at home, but I can't help saying that this bowl of healthy cabbage soup is infinitely preferable to our bourgeois spaghetti."

"Comrade," muttered Peppone, "after the trick you played this morning, you deserve a soup made of boiled nails and arsenic."

"This one is just about as good," retorted Don Camillo.

But as usual, the vodka and roast mutton were highly satisfactory and Peppone was inspired to make a little speech, cast in a conventional mold, to which Comrade Oregov made an equally conventional reply. Luckily Don Camillo was in top form, buoyed up by two glasses of liquid fire and the heart-warming experience of the morning. From a ramp built of quotations from Marx, Lenin and Khrushchev he launched an oratorical sputnik which sent even Comrade Nadia Petrovna into a state of perceptible ecstasy as she translated it and caused the eyes of Comrade Yenka Oregov to shine with a reflected glow.

Don Camillo spoke of the *kolkhos* as if it were a living, breathing being, and his hearers got a new and agreeable feeling that they were happy and important people. After he had reached an operatic conclusion, Comrade Oregov leaped up and pumped his hand interminably, talking all the while in a rapid-fire patter.

"Comrade Oregov says that the Party needs men like you for its rural propaganda," Comrade Petrovna told him, "and he wishes that you would stay here. We have accelerated courses for learning Russian."

"Please thank Comrade Oregov on my behalf," answered Don Camillo. "After I have gone home and had time to make arrangements for my wife and children I may take him up on his offer."

"He says that you can have all the time you want," Comrade Petrovna assured him. "You can count on him to facilitate your return."

More vodka was brought to the table, and the visitors did not get away until the middle of the afternoon.

The torrential rain had transformed the road into a river of mud and the bus had some difficulty getting started. After five miles or so they came to the crossing of the road leading back toward the "Red Flag" *sovkos*. The irrigation canal running alongside had overflowed and the road was under a good fifteen inches of water. With Comrade Oregov's authorization the driver took a left turn in the direction of Tifiz and for a couple of hours the truck rolled over a narrow, winding track which was blessed with a solid bottom.

Unfortunately it began to rain again and the driver was faced with further trouble. The bus skidded from one side to the other, threatening to go off the road, and under continuous abuse the differential got out of order. The rain

gave no indication of letting up and darkness was beginning to fall. Since the village of Tifiz was only two or three
miles away the driver was sent ahead to bring back a tow
truck or a tractor. But he came back with disappointing
news. The only piece of working machinery in Tifiz was attached to the grain elevator. Since this offered no help out
of the present situation and the *kolkhos* at Tifiz belonged to
the distressing six per cent without telephones, the group
had no choice but to walk the rest of the way. They set out,
with a bitter wind blowing into their backs and mud up to
their ankles.

By the time they came to the village it was completely
dark, and since it was one of the unfortunate eight per cent
without electric light, its aspect was anything but welcoming. The assembly room of the rural soviet was filled with
sacks of fodder, but in a voice of unprecedented volume
and severity Comrade Oregov gave orders that it should be
cleared without delay. A group of men armed with brooms
concluded the cleaning operation, leaving the visitors covered with dust at one end of the room, which had only
kerosene lamps to light it. Don Camillo found himself
standing next to Comrade Tavan, the tenant farmer, and
he proceeded at once to undermine his morale.

"Comrade," he said audibly to Peppone, "do you remember what I said to you about the peasants this morning? At
the *sovkos* which is run directly by the government, everything functioned efficiently. But here, where the *kolkhos*
people manage their own affairs, there is nothing but disaster. Trucks and tractors are not running and the assembly room is used for a storehouse. Isn't it very much the
same at home? At Le Pioppette, where many peasant
houses have been rebuilt since the war, what do you find?
Potatoes in the bathtub; kindling wood and chickens in the
garage, while trucks and tractors rust outside. Believe me,
Comrade, peasants haven't the stuff in them to live as free
men under a socialist regime. All they know how to do is

obey orders. How ridiculous to speak of 'giving the peasants
land'! The land must belong to the State, every square inch
of it. We must set up government-directed *sovkos* until
such time as the peasants have acquired some sense of responsibility."

"That's not the half of it, Comrade," chimed in Scamoggia. "It will take centuries for sense of any kind to pene-
trate their noodles."

The surrounding light was dim, but Tavan's flapping ears
had turned red enough to shine even in complete darkness.
Don Camillo was getting ready to shoot off some more of
his ammunition, but the heel of Peppone's right shoe came
down on a corn on his left foot. If a gun barrel had been
stuck into his belly, Don Camillo would have had no
thought of surrender. But a corn irritated by a long walk
in wet weather was strongly conducive to silence.

As the dust subsided, Comrade Oregov was seen standing with his legs wide apart in the middle of the room, is-
suing imperative orders. Trestles and boards were assem-
bled to make a long table. Someone brought out a roll of
burlap, and soon the table had a cloth upon it. Heat began
to fan out of the stove, extra kerosene lamps provided more
light and the table was set with plates, knives, forks, spoons
and glasses. Comrade Oregov glanced at the corner where
Peppone and his little band were awkwardly standing and
guessed at the growing tension among them. In the twinkling of an eye he summoned three girls to pass around the
vodka. After two good drinks the visitors' faith in the ulti-
mate triumph of socialism was fully restored. That is, except in Don Camillo, whom the vodka cast into a deep depression.

Because they were prey to a genuinely Communist hun-
ger they fell like wolves upon the bowls of steaming cab-
bage-and-potato soup. When he saw that their appetites
were satisfied, Comrade Oregov called upon Comrade
Petrovna to express his deep regret for the inconveniences

of the afternoon. Don Camillo was once more in a diabolical mood and he stood up to respond to the apology.

"Actually we have enjoyed the adventure," he began, "because Comrade Oregov gave us a splendid example of how a Communist leader should behave. In my country there is a proverb which says that the master's pride lends nobility to his horse. In our era of mechanization and social progress, which has swallowed up both horse and master, it might be more apt to say that Comrade Oregov is ennobled by the rightful pride which the Communist Party takes in his achievement."

Comrade Oregov was delighted with this witticism and with the compliment which Don Camillo had paid him.

Peppone, as a senator, a Party official and leader of the mission, carried a brief case bulging with important secret papers. In the course of the dinner he imprudently put the brief case down on the floor, and Don Camillo, who was as usual sitting beside him, had an opportunity to open it and quickly examine the contents. Underneath the papers he found a bottle of brandy and a piece of excellent salami. Peppone became aware of his neighbor's discovery only when he quite unexpectedly heard Comrade Oregov thanking him for his generous gifts and insisting upon dividing them among all those present. The gifts, of course, were the bottle of brandy and the salami.

"Comrade," said Don Camillo, when he came back from making the presentation, "that was a splendid gesture. Just as splendid as the round of vodkas which you offered us with the change from your ten-thousand-lira bill."

Peppone shot him an angry look.

"He who laughs last laughs best," he retorted. "We have a long way to go before we get home."

Comrade Oregov was sitting at one end of the long table. At his right were the director and political secretary of the

kolkhos and at his left Comrade Nadia Petrovna. Beside
Comrade Petrovna was Comrade Salvatore Capece of
Naples, who had wedged himself in between her and Com-
rade Nanni Scamoggia.

The brandy and salami showed typical bourgeois inertia
and never got away from this end of the table.

"Comrade," said Capece, turning the full force of his
melting eyes upon Comrade Petrovna, "if I had a guitar I
could make a far prettier speech than that of Comrade
Tarocci."

Comrade Petrovna said something to the director of the
kolkhos, and he disappeared from the table. Nobody noticed, because the heat of the room, the vodka and the cigarette smoke had reduced the whole company to a state of
somnolent euphoria. But when he came back, they were
aroused by a loud shriek from the throat of Comrade
Capece.

"It's a guitar!"

The *kolkhos* of Tifiz did not have a single working machine, but it did have a guitar, and also an accordion with
a boy who knew fairly well how to play it. While Comrade
Capece was tuning the guitar, the boy struck up a march
on the accordion. At this moment the habitually taciturn
tenant farmer, Tavan, had a sudden inspiration. He
snatched the accordion from the boy's hands and sounded
a chord which reduced the whole company to silence. Then
he played *The Horsefly* and *The Mazurka of Migliavacca,*
and played them so well that the size of his ears became almost unnoticeable.

Comrade Salvatore Capece was ready to join in, and to
the accompaniment of the accordion he burst into song. He
sang *O sole mio,* and all of Naples was in his voice, from
the Vomero to Posillip, from Zi' Teresa to *Funiculi, funi-
cula,* from moonlight on the Bay to the Problem of the
South. If he hadn't given them an encore they would have
torn him to pieces.

He sang half a dozen more songs, and Comrade Nanni Scamoggia began to foam at the mouth, because the singer never took his eyes off Comrade Nadia Petrovna and she was in a state of obvious enchantment.

Then Comrade Tavan broke into a polka. This had a magic effect. In a second, table and tableware were swept away and anyone who wanted to go on drinking had to take refuge in the adjacent *kolkhos* office, which was also the repository of the vodka. Everybody began to dance and the only one to actually take refuge from the horrendous sight was Don Camillo, who found the picture of Lenin on the office wall to keep him company.

Comrade Salvatore Capece finally tossed aside the guitar and began to dance with Comrade Nadia Petrovna. He held onto her so jealously that when Peppone had something urgent to get translated she had to literally tear out of his arms.

"Comrade," said Peppone when he had drawn her off into a corner, "after a day's hard work a man is entitled to some good, clean fun. And if a fellow is a spoilsport, like Comrade Tarocci, and refuses to join in, then he deserves to be punished. Don't you agree?"

"I do," she answered promptly.

"Comrade Tarocci has many of the qualities of leadership, but in his own house his jealous, reactionary wife leads him by the nose. Even now, when he's thousands of miles away from home, he's afraid of letting himself go. He's simply got to join the dance!"

"Leave it to me!" said Comrade Petrovna.

Five minutes later a band of laughing girls burst into the office and pulled Don Camillo out into the main room and onto the dance floor. Peppone thoroughly enjoyed the scene, and while Don Camillo was being whirled about by the prettiest of the girls he signaled to Comrade Vittorio Peratto, the photographer from Turin, who whipped out his flash-camera and snapped a sensational picture. After that every one of the girls wanted to have her picture taken dancing with Don Camillo, and when the roll was finished Peppone said to Comrade Peratto:

"You're responsible to me for the negatives, and don't you forget it!"

There was a short pause while the windows were thrown open to clear the room of smoke, and fresh bottles of vodka were uncorked. But the gaiety did not subside. Comrade Li Friddi, the Sicilian, produced a mouth organ; Comrade Curullu, the Sardinian, gave an imitation of a drunk trying to fit a key in a keyhole in an attempt to sneak back into his house late at night; Comrade Gibetti, the Tuscan, sang an operatic air in a shrill falsetto voice, and Comrade Bacciga, from Genoa, held the whole company spellbound with a bag of magician's tricks.

"Organized recreational groups and television have raised the cultural level of the working class," Don Camillo said pantingly to Peppone.

"No doubt about it," Peppone replied. "And I have an idea that back home a display of picture postcards would be much better propaganda than any number of political manifestos."

"What sort of pictures?" inquired Don Camillo.

"Pictures of our beloved parish priest in false clothing, kicking up his heels at a dance."

"Don't count your chickens before they're hatched," retorted Don Camillo. "As you said yourself, we have a long way to go before we get back home!"

The dancing had resumed, and a little man about forty years old accosted Don Camillo.

"Comrade," he said in Italian, "are you the head of the group?"

"No, this stuffed clown beside me is the head. I'm only the cell leader."

"Well, I have something to tell you both. If your Neapolitan friend over there doesn't let go of that girl, the fellow from Rome is going to break his bones."

Without pausing to find out how the stranger happened to speak Italian, Peppone rushed away to forestall any possible trouble. Don Camillo made some wild gesture, and the stranger laughed and showed that he understood.

"Vodka, that's what you want, isn't it?" he inquired.

"Da, da!" responded Don Camillo, still unable to believe that the man spoke his language. And he pointed toward the office, which was also the vodka cellar.

Once they were in the office they were able to talk freely.

"I am a Rumanian," the stranger informed Don Camillo.

"Then how do you happen to speak Italian with a Neapolitan accent?"

"Because I come from Naples, that's why. In 1939 I was a sailor, and I met a Rumanian girl and followed her to Rumania."

"Did you catch up with her?" asked Don Camillo.

"I caught up with her, all right, but not in time."

"What do you mean? Was it too late? Had she already married another man?"

"No, it was too soon, and I had to marry her myself. Fortunately the war came along and the Russians moved into Rumania. They were recruiting agricultural workers and I volunteered to go. . . ."

While the stranger was telling his story, Peppone was waiting for a chance to get hold of Comrade Petrovna. At the end of a mazurka he took her away from Comrade Capece and whirled her into a waltz.

"Look here, Comrade," he said; "I have something to tell you. Comrade Scamoggia is an asset to the Party, but he isn't politically mature. He's subject to capitalistic errors. . . ."

"I've noticed them," said Comrade Petrovna. "But I think he'll outgrow them with time."

"I quite agree. But tonight they have taken the upper hand, and if you don't stop dancing with that guitar player, he may make trouble. I thought I'd tip you off, because I'm sure you wouldn't want the party to wind up in a fight."

They finished the waltz together and then parted company. Peppone went to the office, and Don Camillo brought him up to date on the Neapolitan's story.

"He's never been mixed up in politics," he explained. "He just wants us to help him get out of hot water."

Peppone shrugged his shoulders.

"He went looking for trouble, didn't he? Why didn't he stay in Rumania?"

"Because of my wife," the stranger explained. "I had to get away from her. And it's easier for a Neapolitan to be a Rumanian in Russia than it is in Rumania! I could be perfectly happy here, because I'm a barber and hairdresser, the only one for miles around. I go from one *kolkhos* to another, giving shaves and haircuts. But my real specialty is permanent waves. . . ."

"Permanent waves?"

"Women are women the world over, Chief, and if they have a chance to pretty themselves up they'll starve themselves to death to pay for it. As soon as one girl got a permanent, all the rest of them wanted one, too. My reputation spread like wildfire. . . ."

"I see," said Peppone. "But that doesn't explain why you're in hot water."

"Chief, can't you imagine what it is to be a young man in the middle of this enormous Russia? It's not true what they say about free love. When I came here from Rumania, I had that idea in mind. But if you start flirting with a Russian's wife or his girl, he'll beat you up just as promptly as the next one. At the first *kolkhos* I went to I was caught red-handed and kicked out in no time flat. At the second

I had the same bad luck, and so on, right down the line."

"Well, why worry?" laughed Peppone. "Aren't there eighty thousand *kolkhos* to choose from?"

"Yes, but I'm only one man!" the barber retorted.

Peppone couldn't stop laughing, and Don Camillo decided to take advantage of his good humor.

"The poor fellow's joking," he put in. "The truth is he's crazy to get back to Naples. Can't we give him a hand?"

"What do you mean? We can't take him back in a suitcase, can we?"

"No. But Comrade Rondella was sent home, and you have traveling papers for a group of eleven."

"You're crazy! Under Comrade Oregov's eagle eye?"

"He can't keep tabs on us forever."

"Don't be a fool," said Peppone. "The fellow can stay here and pursue his barber's trade and let the married women alone."

"I don't call that Communism!" said the barber.

"It's a funny story," admitted Peppone, "but I refuse to get mixed up in it." And he went out of the room.

"Don't desert me," the barber implored Don Camillo. "I'm not asking you to get yourself in trouble. Just tell me where you're going and when. I can get myself kicked from one place to another. Only God Almighty can stop a Neapolitan from going home, and Khrushchev isn't God."

Don Camillo copied out the tour schedule.

"That's all I can do for you," he said. "And forget that we ever met. I've forgotten it already."

The main room was more tumultuous than ever and Peppone was searching desperately for Comrade Petrovna. He was desperate because Comrade Capece and Comrade Scamoggia had disappeared also. Finally he caught sight of the girl and grabbed her by the arm.

"What's happened?" he asked her.

"I got there too late," she admitted. "They went out

together and by the time I overtook them it was all over."

"Where is Capece?"

"In the haystack of Barn No. 7."

"And Scamoggia?"

"He's holding a cold compress to Capece's black eye."

"Nobody else knows about it?"

"Only Comrade Capece, who has the black eye for a souvenir, and Comrade Nadia Petrovna, who got slapped in the face!" She clenched her fists angrily. "He had the nerve to hit me!" she added.

This was no laughing matter. Comrade Petrovna was not an ordinary woman; she was high up in the Party and a government employee.

"I quite understand," said Peppone gravely. "Shall I beat him up or shall I report him to Comrade Oregov?"

"There are times when personal feelings have to be sacrificed for the good of the Party," replied Comrade Petrovna. "Just let the whole thing go. Comrade Scamoggia is still under the influence of vodka. When he comes to himself he'll see the stupidity of his behavior."

Peppone shook his head.

"Comrade, Lenin has instructed us to tell the truth, no matter how disagreeable it may be. I happen to know that Scamoggia didn't have a single drop of either vodka or brandy. He wasn't drunk; he knew perfectly well what he was doing."

Comrade Petrovna looked more beautiful than ever and her eyes shone as if with tears. One cheek was slightly redder than the other and she covered it with her hand.

"Comrade," she said humbly, "it's not easy for me to admit, but I'm afraid I too am not politically mature."

Don Camillo suddenly appeared at Peppone's side.

"Anything wrong?" he queried.

"No, everything's in good order," said Peppone sternly.

10

Three Stalks of Wheat

During the night a furious wind out of nowhere swept over the plains and froze the soggy ground over. Don Camillo was the first to wake up, roused by the stentorious snoring of Peppone. Long icicles hung at the windows, but an agreeable warmth came out of the big stove. All around, on improvised cots, his eight companions, overcome by the vodka and uproarious gaiety of the night before, lay in a deep sleep. Don Camillo, like all the rest, had slept with all his clothes on, and Peppone lay on the cot next to his own.

"If he didn't snore so shamelessly," Don Camillo thought to himself, "I'd be almost sorry to have given him so many headaches."

He looked around and silently called the roll. Yes, except for Comrade Yenka Oregov and Comrade Nadia Petrovna, they were all there, and Comrade Salvatore Capece still had a wet compress over his black eye.

"Lord," said Don Camillo, "have pity on these poor fellows and shed light upon their darkness."

He lowered his legs over the edge of the cot and started to put on his shoes. He got the left one on all right, but the right one seemed stuck to the floor. Apparently the lace was caught in a crack. He gave it a hard jerk, and Peppone

99

suddenly stopped snoring. The reason for this coincidence was the simple fact that Peppone had tied Camillo's shoe-lace around his ankle.

"Comrade," Don Camillo said to him reproachfully, "I can't see why you mistrust me."

"After all the tricks you've played under my waking eyes, who knows what you might do while I'm asleep!"

They went to wash up at a pump outside. The icy wind slashed their faces and the inhabitants of the thatch-roofed houses all seemed to have shut themselves up inside. But suddenly there were signs of life. A big truck arrived, and Comrade Oregov, with a group of local men, suddenly appeared on the scene to greet it. Peppone and Don Camillo went to join them.

A boy jumped down from the truck and asked for help in unloading a motorcycle. Then the driver got out and reported to Comrade Oregov. When he turned down his fur coat collar they saw that he was none other than Citizen Stephan Bordonny. The boy had ridden on the motorcycle to get mechanical assistance from Grevinec, and now the visitors' bus driver, accompanied by Comrade Nadia Petrovna, came to see what was to be done next.

"Don't worry," Comrade Petrovna said to Peppone, after Comrade Oregov and Bordonny had held a brief consulta-tion. "He has brought over the necessary parts and the bus will soon be repaired."

"Won't they have to tow the bus here?" asked Peppone.

"That's impossible," she told him. "The road is frozen over and the truck is too light for its tires to get a good grip on the ice. They're going to carry out the repairs on the spot."

"I'm a mechanic myself," said Peppone. "If you'll give me a pair of overalls, I'll be glad to lend a hand."

Comrade Oregov was pleased with this offer, and Com-rade Petrovna told Peppone that a pair of overalls would be provided.

"Make it two pairs," said Peppone. "Comrade Tarocci here is mechanically minded, and we can use his help."

Comrade Oregov approved of this plan and went off on the motorcycle to the neighboring village of Drevinka, whence he intended to notify his superiors by telephone of the forced delay.

"Comrade," Peppone said to Comrade Petrovna, "that leaves you in charge of the rest of the group. If any of them misbehaves, don't hesitate to discipline him. I call Comrade Scamoggia to your particular attention, because he's a troublemaker."

"I thought all night long about the way he insulted me," she replied. "He owes me an explanation."

There was a cold look in her eyes, but it was softened by the brand-new permanent wave which the Neapolitan barber had found time to give her hair.

By now the overalls had been found, and Peppone and Don Camillo drove away in the truck. Peppone confided to Don Camillo that he was alarmed by Comrade Petrovna's formidable air.

"That woman is in a dangerous frame of mind. She's quite capable of taking up lipstick and nail polish, if she can lay her hands on them."

"I don't doubt it," Don Camillo replied. "When it comes to politics, women are always extremists."

During the ride in the truck Citizen Bordonny did not open his mouth and behaved as if he could not understand what his two Italian passengers were saying. The bus driver had climbed in the back, lain down and fallen asleep, but Bordonny was not taking any chances.

Bordonny had brought all the necessary tools, and as soon as they reached the stranded bus he saw what was to be done. The rear end of the bus was easy to jack up, but in order that the jack shouldn't slip on the ice it was necessary to lay a board for it to stand on. The bus driver flatly refused to crawl underneath. His reluctance was natural enough and Peppone was surprised to hear Bordonny argue so violently with him. He tried to put in a word, but Bordonny went on shouting and finally the bus driver turned around and walked away in the direction of the *kolkhos*.

"To hell with him!" Bordonny muttered when the other had gone.

"I don't know that he's to blame," said Peppone, shaking his head. "He just didn't want to risk being pinned down under the bus."

"Bawling him out was the only thing I could do to get him out of the way," Bordonny explained.

Soon the truck was jacked up and work begun. While Bordonny was loosening screws and taking off nuts, he talked to his companions.

"This was the site of a fierce battle just before my capture, around Christmas of 1942. The Russians attacked in overwhelming numbers and when we retreated we left many of our dead behind. A group of some thirty artillerymen and *bersaglieri* were surrounded and taken prisoner, many of them wounded or sick. The Russians shut them up in a barn at a *kolkhos* near the one you've just visited at Tifiz, and when we retook the area a day later we found them dead. The Russians had machine-gunned them rather than let them get away. I was right there when the bodies were discovered, and it was a terrible sight."

Don Camillo and Peppone went on working, although their fingers were numb with cold.

"We gathered up the dead bodies and buried them," Bordonny continued. "If you will walk for three quarters of a mile toward the north you'll see a wagon track leading to the right. Just a hundred yards before you actually reach it, there's an irrigation ditch, with an overgrown hedge on one side. If you go a couple of hundred feet along the hedge you'll come to a big oak tree whose trunk is covered with ivy. The burial ground is right there, in the rectangle bounded by the road, the wagon track, the ditch and a line parallel to the road leading from the wagon track to the oak tree."

They worked on for another half hour without speaking.

"I can do the rest alone,'" said Bordonny. "In case anyone comes I'll sound the horn. If you look under the ivy you'll find something there."

Don Camillo walked resolutely away and Peppone had no choice but to follow him. The sky was dark and the wind continued to blow over the bare plain.

"If the wind lets up there'll be snow," said Don Camillo.

"I hope there's enough to snow you under," retorted Peppone.

They broke into a run and soon they came to the ditch. There was a thick coat of ice on the bottom and Don Camillo clambered down onto it to pursue the rest of the way. When they came to the great oak tree, which raised its bare branches toward the dark sky, they climbed up through an opening in the hedge. Before them lay a wide field, still covered with green stalks of wheat.

For a moment they stood still, gazing at the desolation of the scene. Then Don Camillo forced himself to take a few steps forward and with a trembling hand thrust aside the twining ivy. On the trunk of the tree there was carved a date: *Dec. 27, 1942,* and the single word *Italia,* with a cross above it.

Don Camillo let the ivy fall back, while Peppone slowly took off his cap and looked out over the field, thinking of the wooden crosses that were no longer there, of the scattered bones buried in the cold ground.

"Requiem aeternam dona eis, Domine, et lux perpetuus luceat eis. . . ."

Turning around he saw that at the foot of the oak tree,

under the rude cross that Bordonny had carved upon it, Don Camillo was saying the Mass for the Dead.

"Deus, cuius miseratione animae fidelium requiescunt: famulis et famulabus tuis, et omnibus hic et ubique in Christo quiescentibus, da propitius veniam peccatorum; ut a cunctis reatibus absoluti, tecum sine fine laetentur. Per eumdem Dominum. . . ."

The tender stalks of wheat quivered under impact of the wind.

"My son, where are you?"

Peppone remembered the despairing outcry of the headline over a newspaper story he had seen in the last years of the war.

"Where are you, my son?"

Bordonny was intent upon his work, but he kept one ear cocked for any approaching sound. When he heard someone coming from the direction of the *kolkhos,* he sounded his horn as a warning. It was not, as he had feared, the bus driver, but one of the Italians, the fellow with the big ears. He was walking very slowly and as soon as he drew near, Bordonny halted him.

"Lend me a hand, Comrade, until the others return."

Tavan took off his coat and fell willingly to work, and meanwhile Peppone and Don Camillo hurriedly retraced their way. When they got to the bus, Peppone said to Tavan:

"Hand that tool over to me."

Comrade Tavan wiped his hands on a rag and put on his overcoat. He hung about Don Camillo, who had lit a cigar butt, and finally got up his courage to say:

"Comrade, if you're not busy, I'd like a word with you."

"The experts have taken over," Don Camillo replied. "There's no reason why we can't talk." And they started walking up the road together.

"Comrade," said Comrade Tavan with a slightly embarrassed air. "You have said a great many true things, with which I have to agree. But I can't go along with you when you condemn the whole peasant class. In the city, workers are thrown together; they are in contact with modern progress and in the center of the political scene. Whereas peasants live in isolation and can't be expected to have any community feeling. It's hard to get new ideas into their heads; most often they don't understand them. But a few of them have caught on and are trying to improve their lot."

Comrade Tavan's dark-skinned, bony face and his flapping ears were somehow disarming.

"I know that you're a loyal and hard-working Party man," said Don Camillo. "Perhaps I spoke too hastily. In any case, I didn't mean to wound your class pride."

"You were right," the other replied. "The peasant class is just about the way you describe it, but it's in the process of change. It's the old people who are still holding it back, and in the country old people carry a lot of weight. They have all sorts of wrong ideas, but because they've worked like dogs all their life long, it's hard to contradict them. The Party has all the answers, but the old people still hold the reins. It appeals to their reason, but they listen to their hearts. Even when they are capable of thinking clearly their hearts still rule over their heads."

"Comrade, I'm from peasant stock myself and I know exactly what you mean. That's the peasant problem in a nutshell. And that's why we must step up our propaganda."

They walked on without speaking.

"Comrade," Tavan said abruptly, "my wife and children and I live with my father, who is seventy-five years old, and my mother, who is seventy-three. Our family has been settled on the same piece of land for over a century. My father and mother don't go into the village more than once a year and they've only once been to a big city. How am

I to straighten out their ideas, especially after what happened to them . . . ?"

Don Camillo looked questioningly at him.

"Comrade, if there's anything on your mind, come out with it. You're talking man to man, not to the Party."

Comrade Tavan shook his head.

"I had a brother five years younger than myself," he explained, "and he died in the war. My father managed to accept it, but my mother has never been reconciled. When she heard that I was making this trip she was beside herself, and I had to promise to do what she asked."

"Where was your brother killed?" asked Don Camillo.

"He went where they sent him," said Tavan, "and he was killed right here, in the battle that took place around Christmas of 1942." There was obvious relief in his voice. "My mother made me promise that I'd do everything I could to find the cross that marks his grave and put this in front of it. . . ."

And out of his pocket he pulled a wax votive candle.

"I understand, Comrade," said Don Camillo. "But how can you hope to find the place where he is buried?"

Tavan drew a faded photograph out of his wallet.

"Here it is," he replied. "The regimental chaplain gave this to my mother. There's the cross with my brother's name, and on the back are the name of the nearest village and a local map."

Don Camillo turned the photograph over and then gave it back to him.

"Don't you see, Comrade?" asked Tavan anxiously. "It's right around here, and somehow I must find it. But how can I ask these people to tell me?"

They had walked quite a piece up the road and by now they were not far from the irrigation ditch and the oak tree, the very one that was marked on the map.

"Walk faster," said Don Camillo, at the same time quickening his own pace. When they came to the ditch he halted.

"This is the road, here's the ditch with the hedge running along it, and there's the tree." And followed by Comrade Tavan he retraced his way along the bottom of the ditch and climbed out of it just below the oak. "There," he said, pointing at the wheat field, "this is the place where your brother lies."

He lifted up the ivy and showed him the cross and the date carved on the bark of the tree. Comrade Tavan looked out over the field, and the hand that was holding the candle trembled. Don Camillo took a few steps forward, bent down and dug a hole in the earth. Tavan understood and put the candle into the hole and lighted it. Then he stood up and stared straight ahead, holding his cap in his hand. Don Camillo took a knife from his pocket and cut out a clod of earth with three slender stalks of wheat growing in it. He put the clod in the aluminum cup which he always carried with him for use as a chalice. "I'll get hold of another cup somehow," he told himself. And he said to Tavan:

"Take this to your mother."

Then they walked back to the edge of the field.

"Make the sign of the cross, Comrade," said Don Camillo. "I'm going to do the same thing myself."

From where they stood they could see the flickering flame of the votive candle.

Then the sound of the horn caused them to hasten their steps back to the bus. Just before they got there Don Camillo stopped.

"Comrade," he said, "your mother will be happy, but the Party can't possibly approve."

"I don't give a damn about the Party," said Comrade Tavan emphatically.

And he fingered the cup containing the clod of earth and the stalks of wheat as tenderly as if they were alive.

11

The Cell Goes to Confession

THERE WERE FEW PASSENGERS aboard the train for Moscow and soon Don Camillo found himself alone in a compartment. When Peppone saw him pull out the famous book of excerpts from Lenin he went off in disgust to chat with Comrade Nadia Petrovna and Comrade Yenka Oregov, who had set up their headquarters at the front end of the car. Don Camillo put away the disguised breviary and took out his notebook.

"Thursday, 8 A.M. Tifiz *kolkhos*. Stephan Bordonny. War cemetery. Mass for the Dead. Comrade Tavan. 3 P.M. Departure by train."

Thursday? Was it only Thursday? He could hardly believe that he had been in the Soviet Union for no more than seventy-nine hours.

Once more darkness was falling, and not a single tree or house broke the monotony of the wind-swept plain. There were only endless wheat fields, which in his mind's eye he could picture green and alive under the summer sun. But no amount of imagination was sufficient to warm his heart. He thought of the winter landscape of his native Bassa, with its heavy fog, drenched fields and muddy roads. There no wind was too icy to extinguish the natural warmth generated by the touch of man. A peasant trudging through that landscape did not feel cut off from the rest of the world. Invisible life-giving threads bound him to his fellows. Here there were no such bonds. A man was like a brick in a wall, a necessary but interchangeable part of the national structure. At any moment he might be discarded and thrown on the scrap heap, and then he had no reason to go on living. Here, in short, man was desperately isolated and alone. Don Camillo shuddered. Then he was roused by the thought:

"Where the devil is that rascal Peppone?"

The door of the compartment creaked, and he saw the inquiring face of Comrade Tavan.

"Am I disturbing you?" Tavan asked.

"Come on in and sit down," replied Don Camillo.

Tavan sat down on the opposite seat. He took a roll of cardboard out of his pocket, and after a moment's hesitation showed it to his companion.

"Only a few more days and they won't have to suffer any longer," he explained, pointing to the cup containing the three stalks of wheat, which he had concealed inside. "They can get air from the open end of the tube. Do you think I ought to punch holes in the side as well?"

"No, I think they're quite all right the way they are. The important thing is not to let them get overheated."

Tavan stood the tube up against the back of the seat.

"But later on. . . ." he began.

"Later on? When do you mean?"

"When I'm back home. . . ."

Don Camillo shrugged his shoulders.

"Comrade, I don't see anything difficult about transplanting three stalks of wheat."

"The difficulty's with my mother," said Tavan. "What am I going to say? 'This is some wheat that . . .'?" He paused and looked out the window. "With eleven million square miles of land why did they have to sow wheat in that particular place?" he muttered.

Don Camillo shook his head.

"Comrade," he said, "if a country has twenty million war dead of its own, it can't make much ado over the fifty or a hundred thousand left on its soil by the enemy."

"That's not something I can tell my mother," objected Tavan.

"I'm not recommending it. Let your mother go on thinking about the wooden cross which the photograph showed over her son's grave. Tell her that you lit the candle in front of it. As for the three stalks of wheat, do whatever your heart prompts you. If you keep them alive and transplant them, then their seed will somehow keep alive the memory of your brother."

Tavan listened with a gloomy air and Don Camillo changed the subject.

"Comrade," he said, "what makes you raise such sentimental and bourgeois questions?"

"I like to discuss them," said Tavan, picking up the roll of cardboard and starting to go away. Before leaving he looked again out of the window.

"Eleven million square miles, and they had to pick on that one acre. . . ." he repeated.

Don Camillo did not remain long alone. A few minutes later the door swung open again and Comrade Bacciga from Genoa came in. He sat down across from Don Camillo and because he was a hard-headed, direct sort of fellow he came straight to the point.

"Comrade," he said, "I've been thinking things over, and I see that you're in the right. This is no place to make deals in minks and nylons. And I'm sorry for the stupid things I said after you'd denounced me."

"I owe you an apology, too," said Don Camillo. "I should have talked to you man to man instead of bringing the matter up in front of the whole cell. But the fact is that

Comrade Oregov had seen what you were up to, and I
wanted to clear it up before he did."

Comrade Bacciga mumbled something under his breath
and then said:

"He got the stole, didn't he, even if the deal was illegal?"

"At least the story went no farther," said Don Camillo
consolingly.

"Yes, but I got the short end of the deal," said Bacciga.

"You paid for your fun, that's all, Comrade," said Don
Camillo.

"But what am I going to say to the person who gave me
the stockings and told me to bring back the mink stole in
return . . . ?" He went on grumbling under his breath
and then added: "Comrade, let's be frank. Last night I saw
the trick the senator played on you and I heard him saying
you have a bossy wife. Well, my wife is ten times as bad,
I can tell you. She's the one that got me into it, and if I
don't bring back the goods not even Comrade Togliatti
himself can save me. I can't haul her up in front of the
Party organization, because she's a stinking Fascist as well.
Her daughters will take her side, and they're even worse
than she is."

"Stinking Fascists, too?" inquired Don Camillo.

"Worse than that! They're Christian Democrats. Storm
troopers, I call them!"

"I understand," said Don Camillo. "How can I help you?"

"Comrade, I work on the docks, and so I always manage
to have a few American dollars in my pocket. America
stinks, too, but dollars always come in handy. Do you get
the point?"

"Not exactly, no."

"Comrade, for the sake of keeping peace at home I'm
willing to part with my dollars. Is there anything wrong
about that?"

"About your spending your dollars? Not a thing. The
Soviet Union needs dollar exchange."

"I thought so," said Bacciga with relief. "And while we're about it, can you give me an idea of what they're worth?"

Don Camillo was thoroughly informed.

"The official exchange is four rubles for a dollar, but tourists are entitled to ten. Reactionary papers claim that there's a black market as well, and you can get twenty. But of course that's the usual anti-Communist propaganda."

"Of course," said Bacciga. "So once we get to Moscow I can do what I like with my money, is that it?"

"It's perfectly legitimate, Comrade."

Comrade Bacciga went away satisfied, but Don Camillo had no time to make a note of what had happened because Comrade Salvatore Capece was already at the door. The cold compress had been effective and his left eye was now circled with only a rim of pale blue.

"Comrade," he said, sitting down across from Don Camillo, "I don't know how you do it, but you gulp down that vodka as if it were brandy. But it's still vodka. There's no telling what it may do to you, and after the mischief is done, well, it's irrevocable."

Don Camillo nodded assent, and the other went on:

"The senator told me that he'd settle with me later. Meanwhile I have a black eye and a lump as big as a nut on the back of my neck. What more of a settlement can he want? My wife's active in our local Party cell, and if there's any talk about all this foolishness she's sure to hear about it. She's hot-blooded and jealous. I needn't say any more, because it seems that you have to cope with very much the same thing."

"Don't worry, Comrade," said Don Camillo; "I'll take it up with the senator myself."

Capece leaped to his feet with a look of obvious relief.

"Salvatore Capece, that's my name!" he exclaimed. "If you ever come to Naples, just ask for Salvatore Capece. Everyone there knows me!"

By now so much had happened that Don Camillo felt he really must jot it down. But fate would not have it that way. Before he could pull out his notebook Comrade Peratto blew in. As a Piedmontese from Turin he lost no time beating around the bush.

"Comrade," he said, "yesterday we had quite a bit of fun. That's always the way when there's drinking. But now the effects of the vodka are gone and I'm cold sober. The senator can say what he likes, but I'm a professional photographer, not an amateur. And so here's the roll containing all the pictures I snapped last night. Do what you want with them."

Don Camillo accepted the roll.

"I'm grateful, Comrade. It's very decent of you."

"It's a matter of professional ethics," said Comrade Peratto, preparing to take his leave, "and also of masculine solidarity. My own wife is growing more jealous every day. I'll tell the senator the film was exposed to the light."

After Peratto had gone Don Camillo lifted his eyes to heaven. "Lord," he said, "after all this I'm almost ashamed of not having a jealous wife." Then he took out his notebook and wrote down: *"Wives are the opium of the people."* Before he could add anything more Comrade Scamoggia appeared at the door. He threw himself down on the seat across from Don Camillo's, lit a cigarette and then let it hang from one corner of his down-turned mouth. He looked unusually serious and it was plain that there was something on his mind. Don Camillo looked at him inquiringly for a moment, and then as the other gave no signs of speaking he decided to complete his notes.

"Comrade!" Scamoggia interrupted, and Don Camillo hurriedly put the notebook away.

"Something wrong?" he asked innocently.

"Comrade, you know what happened last night," Scamoggia began.

"Have no fear about that," Don Camillo reassured him.

"Capece was just here, and everything's in good order."

"Capece? What's he got to do with it?" said Scamoggia, very much surprised.

"He got the black eye, didn't he?" exclaimed Don Camillo.

"Oh, perhaps he did," said Scamoggia distractedly. "That's not what I came to talk about."

"Then I'm completely in the dark," said Don Camillo. Scamoggia puffed the cigarette smoke slowly out of his mouth.

"Last night, in a moment of weakness, I hit somebody in the face."

"Yes, I know," said Don Camillo impatiently.

"Oh, I don't mean Comrade Capece. I mean the girl." Don Camillo was thoroughly taken aback.

"You mean to say you hit Comrade Petrovna? How could you do a thing like that?"

Comrade Scamoggia threw out his arms as if to indicate that he himself could give no explanation.

"Comrade Petrovna is an intelligent woman," said Don Camillo. "She'll understand that it was all on account of the vodka."

"I hadn't been drinking, and she knows it," said Scamoggia. "That's the whole trouble." He threw his cigarette on the floor and stamped it out. Don Camillo had never seen him in such a state of depression.

"Don't be melodramatic, Comrade," he said. "She's a lovely girl."

"Exactly," said Scamoggia. "She's worth her weight in gold, and I can't treat her as if she were just a casual pickup. I have no right to lead her on."

Don Camillo's country, La Bassa, was hundreds of miles from Rome and he couldn't fathom the workings of Scamoggia's city-slicker mind.

"Lead her on?" he said. "What do you mean?"

"It's no joke!" shouted the Roman heartbreaker. "When

Nanni Scamoggia hits a girl in the face, it's not without some reason. Do I look to you like the kind of man that roughs up a woman just for the fun of it?"

Don Camillo shook his head.

"I see. You're afraid the girl has got the idea that you're seriously interested in her."

"Exactly."

"You don't want to get married, is that it, and you're afraid to tell her."

"That's it."

"Then it's perfectly simple. Just let things coast along, and in three days, when you go home, she'll realize that she has to get over it."

"But *I* won't get over it. That's the point."

Don Camillo saw that the situation was even more complex than he had imagined.

"In that case I can't give you any advice," he admitted.

"Yes, you can. You know how to think straight, and I'm counting on you. We had a long talk last night, after it was all over. I had to explain."

"Quite right."

"In a few months she'll be coming to Rome as interpreter to a guided tour. And then . . ." And after a moment of hesitation he added: "Comrade, can I trust you?"

"Just as if you were talking to your confessor."

"I wouldn't be caught dead in the confessional!"

"Quite right," said Don Camillo. "Nevertheless there are priests who have died rather than reveal the substance of a confession. If I were a priest that's the kind I'd be. So you can speak quite freely."

"When she comes to Rome she'd just as soon stay there, in order to be with me. Is it right for me to encourage her?"

"No," said Don Camillo peremptorily. "That would be

dishonorable. A Comrade Scamoggia can't behave that way. There's a much more natural and honorable solution."

"What's that?"

"The girl's very good at her job and probably she enjoys the favor of the Party. When we get to Moscow she can doubtless obtain permission for you to stay here. The Soviet Union needs men with strong convictions and technical ability. Once you've settled yourself here the rest will be easy. You can satisfy both your heart and your conscience. Surely that's better than involving an innocent, lovesick girl in an affair in a foreign land."

Scamoggia's face lighted up.

"Comrade, my mind wasn't working and you've set it back on the right track. As you say, it's all quite simple. I'm glad I unburdened myself to you."

And after vigorously shaking Don Camillo's hand he went away.

"Lord," said Don Camillo, "the Comrade shepherd's job is to bring the lost sheep back to the Party fold."

"Not so," said the Lord; "that's the job of Comrade Devil!"

But perhaps this was not the Lord's voice; perhaps it was the voice of the wind howling over the steppes. Don Camillo had to leave the question unanswered because Peppone was standing before him.

"Why haven't you come to talk with us," said Peppone, "instead of sitting here and staring out of the window?"

"Comrade," said Don Camillo gravely. "A cell leader has a lot to do if he's to live up to his Party responsibilities."

Peppone stared at him suspiciously and then shrugged his shoulders. No matter how diabolical his enemy might be, what harm could he do shut up in a compartment of a train traveling through Mother Russia?

12
In the Jaws of Hell

THIS WAS PEPPONE'S GREAT DAY! They had visited a tractor factory and a *kolkhos* and traveled by train for twenty consecutive hours through an endless expanse of fertile, cultivated land. These things had given them some idea of the Soviet Union's agricultural resources and industrial efficiency, but they had not made an overwhelming impression. Indeed, a series of regrettable accidents had tipped the balance in favor of the West. But now, Peppone reflected, all doubts and misconceptions would be swept away; the Western point of view was doomed to annihilation. The luxurious, ultra-modern bus in which they were driving down the broad streets of Moscow was quite unlike the rickety vehicle in which they had been transported across the muddy roads of the Ukraine, and around them were not thatch-roofed hovels but towering skyscrapers. Don Camillo, the disguised representative of the Western point of view, was momentarily speechless.

"Don't let it get you down, Comrade," Peppone whispered into his ear. "Even what you can see with your own eyes is a mirage created by propaganda. Meanwhile, if you want some exercise, you can take a little walk around the Kremlin. The circumference only measures three miles."

He was repeating the data furnished by Comrade
Nadia Petrovna, but there was as much pride in his voice
as if he had built Moscow with his own two hands. As
for Comrade Yenka Oregov, the visitors' admiring exclama-
tions made him tremulous with joy. He was no cold and
indifferent bureaucrat; in return for his salary of a thousand
rubles a month he gave at least ten thousand rubles' worth
of zeal and enthusiasm. He was happy in the conviction
that he was a humble but essential part of the gigantic
structure of the Communist State. "It takes a hundred
kopeks to make a ruble and a thousand times a thousand
rubles to make a million rubles. But without my kopek the
million rubles would not be complete." This was the way
he saw it, and his reasoning was not as absurd as it might
have seemed, because the investment of a single kopek
gave him the feeling that he was a millionaire. The visitors'
gaping admiration filled him with pride, but when he saw
that they had digested all they could of the wonders of
Moscow he instructed Comrade Nadia Petrovna to inform
them that the preliminary part of their tour of the city was
over.

"Comrade Oregov says that you may want to stretch
your legs," she announced, "and he advises you to return
by foot to the hotel. It's only a few hundred yards away."

They got out of the bus in the middle of an im-
posing square. As if he had suddenly remembered an
unimportant detail, Comrade Oregov wheeled around and
led them into a small building which housed an escalator.
The next thing they knew they were carried down into
the bowels of the earth.

"Comrades," said Comrade Petrovna, when they got to
the bottom, "this is the subway!"

The famous Moscow subway was grandiose in the Babylonian manner. Everywhere there was decoration: bronze
and marble statuary, bas-reliefs, paintings and gleaming
glass. It seemed almost as if the carpeting must be made

of mink. Peppone and his companions were overpowered, and Comrade Oregov glowed with satisfaction. The first to speak was Comrade Scamoggia.

"Comrade," he said in a subdued voice to Comrade Petrovna, "next to you this is the most gorgeous sight of the Soviet Union!"

She was taken by surprise but recovered herself sufficiently to answer:

"Comrade, this triumph of Soviet art and industry doesn't lend itself to jokes."

"But Comrade, I'm not joking," Scamoggia insisted.

He spoke so earnestly that for a moment Comrade Petrovna forgot her Party dignity and gave him a capitalistic smile. Meanwhile Peppone nudged Don Camillo.

"Comrade," he said with a grin, "can you imagine what that priest with whom we have both had some dealings would say?"

The subway was beginning to be crowded with people: men and women in the usual ill-fitting clothes, with the usual gloomy expression on their faces.

"I know what he'd say," replied Don Camillo. "He'd say that it's better to eat steak out of an earthenware dish than an onion served on a golden platter."

"Materialism of the lowest degree!" said Peppone. But his imagination lingered over the steak.

These were the days of the famous thaw, and the Soviet government had chosen to lodge the visitors in the very best hotel. It was a structure as magnificent as the subway, with over a thousand rooms, elaborate reception halls and elevators in every corner. After lunch Don Camillo sat in an armchair in the lobby to watch the people go by. They were of every race and color: black, brown, yellow and all shades of white, apparently coming from every corner of the globe and jabbering in a variety of languages. Soon the watchful Peppone came to sit down beside him.

"It's like the tower of Babel," remarked Don Camillo.

"So it seems," Peppone agreed. "But although they speak so many different tongues, they manage to understand one another. They all think the same way; that's the power of Communism. Did you notice the crowd we saw this morning standing in line to visit the tomb of Lenin? Because he brought light into darkness, men come from everywhere to pay him their respects."

Don Camillo gazed earnestly at Peppone.

"Comrade, when you were mayor you didn't know any of these things."

"Yes, I did. I knew them just as well as I do now, only I wasn't aware of it. Later I thought them over and crystallized my ideas. It's just what happened when Jesus Christ was in fashion. Only in the case of Christ it was superstition that bound men together, whereas now it's reason. The truth was always there, but it took Lenin to light a torch by which all men could see it. That's why every visitor to Moscow wants more than anything to visit his tomb."

"But isn't there somebody else in there with him?" asked Don Camillo.

"There is and there isn't," said Peppone. "Anyhow, Lenin is the one people come to see. You'll have a chance to look at him yourself."

"No, I won't," said Don Camillo, shaking his head.

"We're going there shortly, all of us," said Peppone. "I've just been talking over plans with Comrade Oregov."

"I have no debt of gratitude to discharge," said Don Camillo. "I don't follow the vagaries of fashion, and for me Christ is still the only true Light."

"But you have duties, as a cell leader."

"My duty as a priest comes first," said Don Camillo. Pulling a postcard out of his pocket, he set it down on a nearby table and began to write.

"I hope you're not up to some more of your tricks," grumbled Peppone.

"Isn't it legitimate for a fellow to have a friend whose address happens to be the Bishopric Square?"

"Except for the fact that nobody besides the Bishop has that address!"

Don Camillo held out the card for inspection.

"That's why I'm able to address it to plain Mr. So-and-so, which happens to be the bishop's name!"

Peppone glared at the card and gave it back to him. "I'm not sticking my nose into your personal affairs."

"Nevertheless, if I were you, I'd add my signature," Don Camillo advised him.

"Are you crazy?"

"What if Christ were to come back into fashion?" insinuated Don Camillo.

Peppone took the card and scribbled his name at the bottom.

"Don't get me wrong," he said sternly. "It's only because your bishop happens to be a very lovable man."

Don Camillo got up and slipped the card into a mail-box attached to a column in the hall. When he came back he found the whole group gathered together.

"According to your wishes," said Comrade Nadia Petrovna, "we're going to visit the tomb of Lenin."

Don Camillo started to go along with the others, but at the door he stumbled and turned his ankle. If Peppone had not braced him with one arm he would have fallen flat on the floor.

"We'll send for the hotel doctor," said Comrade Petrovna. "I trust it's nothing serious, but you'd better stay here and rest."

Don Camillo seemed so very disappointed that Comrade Oregov felt the need to console him.

"You'll be able to visit the tomb another time," he said cheeringly.

And so Don Camillo hobbled back to his chair. He rubbed his ankle and of course it was immediately restored to normal. With a sigh of relief he pulled out of his pocket the famous book of excerpts from Lenin.

A half-hour went by, and Don Camillo was so completely absorbed in his thoughts that he forgot that he was Comrade Tarocci. Just at this point a voice said:

"Father!"

Don Camillo looked up and then kicked himself for his stupidity. But it was too late to cover it up. In the adjacent chair, which had been vacated by Peppone, sat a thin, dark-haired man about forty-five years old. Don Camillo recognized him at once and spontaneously called him by name.

"Comassi!" he exclaimed.

The newcomer held an open copy of *Pravda* before him and leaned over toward Don Camillo as if he were translating an article on the front page for his benefit.

"I knew you the minute I saw you," he explained, "even if you weren't wearing your cassock."

"I wanted to see Moscow," said Don Camillo, "but I had to wear suitable clothes."

"You mean you're still a priest?" the newcomer muttered.

"What else could I be?" said Don Camillo.

"So many people have switched their allegiance. . . ." said the other.

"My allegiance is of a kind that can't be switched. . . . But tell me, what are you doing here?"

"I came with a group of comrades from Prague. That's where I'm living. We go back tomorrow."

"And I suppose you'll report that I'm a Vatican spy."

"Don Camillo, you know me better than that!"

The Comassis were a good churchgoing family from

Castelletto; only young Athos had fallen away. His story was the same as that of many of his contemporaries. On September 8, 1943, when Badoglio signed an armistice with the Allies, he cast off his soldier's uniform and made for home. Then when he was called up to the army of Mussolini's short-lived Fascist republic, he took to the hills. He was not seen again until April of 1945, when the Partisans came out of hiding, and with them many last-minute recruits, who had foresightedly grown long beards in order to appear veterans of the Partisan struggle. Young Comassi wore a red kerchief around his neck and held a position of command. He assumed charge of local operations, which consisted largely of obtaining forced contributions of money from the landowners, each one in proportion to the area of his land. Fists flew and many a landowner was lucky to escape with his life.

Seventy-five-year-old Count Mossoni, together with his seventy-year-old wife, a servant girl and a dog, lived quietly in an isolated manor house in the center of the plain. One morning when their tenant farmer came to deliver a can of milk nobody answered the bell. He walked into the house and found it empty. Only the dog stood in one corner and could not be persuaded to leave it. The farmer called in some neighbors and they found that the dog was standing guard over the rim of an old, indoor well. At the bottom of the well lay the bodies of the count, the countess and the servant girl. Apparently thieves had broken in during the previous night, jimmied open a safe hidden behind a portrait hanging on the second-floor drawing room wall and killed all three human occupants of the house.

A dozen people had seen young Comassi leave the village by car that evening with a group of young toughs and a strange man who was apparently their leader. Other witnesses had noticed the car going up the Mossoni driveway. The three young toughs had kept watch outside while

Comassi and the stranger went in. Twenty minutes later they all drove away together.

These were dangerous times and no one dared come forward and testify against them. For three years the affair was forgotten. But during the elections of 1948 posters were stuck up in the village telling the whole story of the murder and pointing out what kind of men the Reds were trying to put in power. The three young toughs were able to prove that they hadn't gone into the house and claimed they had never known the identity of the stranger. As for Comassi, he had once more disappeared. That is, until this moment, when Don Camillo discovered him at his side.

"What are you doing in Prague?" he asked him.

"They say I have a good voice, and I make news broadcasts in Italian."

"That's a dirty job," said Don Camillo. "Does your family know?"

"No, they don't. But I'd like them to hear my voice and know that I'm alive."

"That wouldn't make them very happy. They're better off thinking that you're dead."

"But I want them to know," Comassi insisted. "That's my whole purpose in speaking to you. God must have meant to give me this chance."

"God! This is a fine time to remember Him! He wasn't in your thoughts when you murdered those poor old people!"

Comassi made an abrupt motion as if there were something he felt impelled to say. Then, apparently, he thought better of it.

"I understand," he murmured. "I can't expect you to believe me. But since you're a priest, you can't refuse to hear my confession."

The hotel lobby was thronged with people of every

race and tongue. Black, brown and yellow faces mingled together and a discordant clamor filled the room. Don Camillo felt as if he were in the jaws of hell, and yet God was there, perhaps more vividly than anywhere else in the world. Christ's words rang in Don Camillo's ear: "Knock and it shall be opened unto you. . . ." He made the sign of the cross and Comassi followed his example, cautiously and deliberately, because there were hundreds of watchful eyes around him, beyond the paper curtain of the *Pravda*.

"O God of infinite mercy, here at Your feet is the sinner who has offended you . . . humbly seeking Your pardon. . . . Lord, do not turn me away . . . do not despise a humble and contrite heart. . . . *Cor contritum et humiliatum non despicies.* . . ."

In an almost inaudible voice Comassi repeated the prayer which Don Camillo recalled to him. Then he said what he had to say, and the words came from his heart, although he seemed to be reading them from the newspaper.

". . . We went in and threatened them with a gun. At first they wouldn't reveal the hiding place, but finally they did. . . . The leader told me to go up to the drawing room on the second floor and take the money while he kept an eye on them. When I came back he was all alone. He took the money, saying that it would all go to the Cause. . . . Then, just before the election, when the posters told the story, they helped me to get away. . . ."

"Why didn't you protest your innocence?"

"I couldn't. He was a higher-up of the Party. . . ."

"Then why don't you come forward now?"

"I can't. It would be even worse now than then. The Party would be involved in a scandal."

"You mean to say that you still respect the Party?"

"No, but I'm afraid. If I said anything they'd liquidate me."

"But what is the leader's name?"

The name was one so much in the news that Don Camillo could hardly believe it.

"Nobody must find out what I have told you, but I want my father and mother to know that I'm not a murderer. That much you can tell them. And I want them to listen to my radio broadcasts, not on account of what I say but simply in order to hear my voice. That way I can feel that I'm still alive, and not just a dead man crying in the wilderness. . . ."

He pulled a sealed envelope out of his pocket and surreptitiously transferred it to the pocket of Don Camillo.

"Here's the whole story, with my signature. You mustn't open the envelope, but you can tell that man that it is in your possession and that I want to go home. . . ."

Comassi was very pale and his voice trembled.

"*Ego te absolvo . . .*" said Don Camillo.

Comassi seemed to have recovered his peace of mind. He folded the newspaper and handed it to Don Camillo.

"You can keep it as a souvenir," he said. "You've never heard a confession in a stranger place than this. . . . Forget what I said to you about the letter; I should never have said it. There's nothing to be done, really. . . . I've passed the point of no return."

"Don't be so sure, Comrade," said Don Camillo. "God still has an outpost in Prague. He's better organized than you may think. Meanwhile I'll see to it that your father and mother listen to your broadcasts, not on account of what you say, but simply in order to hear your voice."

Comassi got up.

"God!" he said. "Who could have imagined that someone would speak to me of God in a place like this?"

"God has outposts everywhere, Comrade," said Don Camillo, "even in Moscow. God's organization is very old, but it's still working."

13

Comrade Nadia's Coffee

"COMRADE, I'm in trouble," said Scamoggia.

"Everyone has to stew in his own juice," replied Don Camillo.

"It's not my own trouble," Scamoggia explained; "It's somebody else's. Only it's been passed on to me and my duty is to pass it on to my immediate superior. Then you'll report it to the chief and he'll report it to the echelon above him. Isn't that the correct official procedure?"

Don Camillo, wearied by the Babylonian tumult of the lobby, had gone upstairs and thrown himself down on his bed.

"If it's an official matter, yes," he said, pulling himself into an upright position. "Sit down and tell me more about it."

Scamoggia shrugged his shoulders.

"I'll give you the story," he said, "and you can decide for yourself how official it is. Do you know Comrade Gibetti?"

"Of course," said Don Camillo.

Actually he knew only what he had read in Peppone's files. Gibetti was a Tuscan, forty years old, an electrical engineer, an active Partisan, well grounded in Party ideology. He had had no occasion to size the fellow up at first hand, because, like the Sicilian Li Friddi and the

127

Sardinian Curullu, Gibetti was close-mouthed and never revealed what he was thinking.

"I like him," said Scamoggia. "He's tough, like myself. And as a Partisan he risked his life without flinching."

"I know that," said Don Camillo.

"Did you know that during the war he fought here in Russia, somewhere near Stalino?"

"In view of his subsequent Partisan record, that's not to be counted against him."

"I agree, Comrade; it shouldn't matter, but in his case it does."

"Why so?"

"During the war he was only twenty-three years old. In spite of instructions he had an urge to fraternize with the enemy. And when the enemy happens to be a stunning seventeen-year-old girl, you can see that the fraternizing might go too far. It did, but then came to retreat, and it was all over."

Don Camillo threw out his arms.

"It's not a pretty story," he said, "but in war such things are bound to happen. In every country there are girls who got themselves into trouble with foreign soldiers."

"Yes," admitted Scamoggia, "but it's unusual to find a soldier who goes on thinking of an enemy girl for seventeen years after the war is over. And that's Gibetti's story." He puffed at his cigarette and then went on: "He told me all about it. Originally he wanted to take the girl home. He dressed her up in an army uniform and with the help of his comrades started to carry out this plan. Then his unit was encircled by the Russians and because he was afraid she might be shot he sent her away. He gave her all the tins of rations that he could get out of his friends and told her to hide out in an abandoned *isba,* where he promised to pick her up again if they escaped from the Russians' clutches. 'But if we're killed or captured,' he said, 'wait until it's all over and then go home. You can say that the Italians carried you away.'

"The battle lasted three days, and at the end the Russians had to beat a retreat for fear of being encircled in their turn. Gibetti returned to the *isba*, but she was no longer there. He went back to Italy with the thought of her still haunting his mind. After the armistice he took to the mountains as a Partisan, but he still hadn't forgotten her. At the end of the war he joined the Party, but even that was no help to him in retracing the girl. All he could do was send letters to her by any Party comrade who went to Russia. Either the letters never got mailed or else they didn't reach their destination; in any case he had no reply. Finally, seventeen years later, he found a chance to come to Russia himself, and at this particularly favorable time when the tension between the two countries is relaxed.

"On our original program we were to visit Stalino, and the girl supposedly lives close by. But there has been a change of plans, and he doesn't know what to do. That's why he told me the story. 'You're on good terms with Comrade Nadia Petrovna,' he said. 'See if you can't do something for me. I'm willing to stay here, if necessary; I'd do anything to find that girl.'

"I told him to leave it to me and trust my discretion. Then I went to Comrade Nadia. She's a woman with a head on her shoulders and the first thing she said was that she must look into the girl's present situation. I gave her the name and address and she wrote to a friend of hers who holds down an important post in Stalino."

Scamoggia paused and took a typewritten sheet from his pocket.

"Here's the reply," he said.

Don Camillo turned the paper over in his hands.

"This doesn't mean anything to me," he said. "I don't know Russian."

"Here's Comrade Nadia's Italian translation," said Sca-moggia, handing him another sheet of paper.

The letter was brief. It said that a Soviet mechanized unit had found the girl, clad in an Italian army coat, at an *isba* near the enemy lines. She claimed that the Italians had brought her there after they had withdrawn from the village of K., against her will, but that she had finally escaped them. She was taken back to K., handed over to the village authorities, accused of collaboration with the enemy and executed on the spot.

"But I can't tell this to Gibetti," Scamoggia concluded. "If you think he ought to be told, go ahead and tell him. If you don't, remember that he's dead set on staying here because he thinks he can find her. It's too much for me, and I'm washing my hands of it."

And he strode out of the room leaving Don Camillo alone. The Soviet Union has more than its share of devils and one of them began tugging at Don Camillo's cassock, the cassock which he still wore in spirit beneath his disguise. The devil whispered: "Go ahead, Don Camillo! Here's your chance to sink Gibetti!" But Don Camillo booted him away. A moment later Peppone came through the door and Don Camillo grabbed his arm.

"After all, you do outrank me," he said, shoving the papers into his hand. "I'm putting this little affair right in your lap."

Then since the papers alone were not sufficient to make his point he proceeded to furnish a full explanation. Peppone turned around to lock the door and then gave vent to his feelings.

"The elite!" he shouted. "Ten hand-picked men! And what do we see? Rondella made trouble from the start and had to be sent home. Scamoggia came with bottles of perfume in his pocket and the idea of playing Don Juan, and Capece went and set himself up as his rival. Bacciga's purpose was to deal on the black market, Tavan's to light

a candle on his brother's grave. Peratto said he was going
to take pictures for the Party paper and on the side he's
selling others to the capitalist press—he thinks he's put
it over on me but I know perfectly well what he's up to.
And now Gibetti, who seemed to be beyond reproach, is
contributing to the confusion! Is it possible that not a
single man came to see the Soviet Union? Has every one
of them got some personal motive up his sleeve?"

"You're too hard on them, Comrade," said Don Camillo
consolingly. "Curullu and Li Friddi are as pure as driven
snow."

"A pair of dummies, that's what they are! They don't
say a word for fear of compromising themselves."

"And then you've forgotten Comrade Taroccil"

"Tarocci?" mumbled Peppone. "Who's that?" Then he
came to himself and stood with his legs wide apart,
wagging his thumb in Don Camillo's face.

"You . . . !" he shouted, "You'll send me home with a
heart attack if you don't watch out!" And he threw himself on his bed in exhaustion. His usual aggressiveness had
crumpled and he could hardly speak. "You're nothing but
a blackmailer! You've got me into such a mess that if it
became known I'd be a laughingstock the world over. Ever
since I ran into you in Rome my life has been hell. Every
time you open your mouth my heart skips a beat and my
stomach turns over. I have nightmares all night long and
when I get up I feel as if all my bones were broken." He
paused to wipe the perspiration from his brow. "If you
wanted to get me down, you can be happy. I'm down and
out."

Don Camillo had never seen Peppone in such a low
state of mind or imagined that he could be at such a
total loss as to what to do. He felt strangely sorry for
him.

"God is witness that I never meant you any harm," he
expostulated.

"Then why did you get me into this play-acting? There's no iron curtain any more. You've seen that there are people from every country in the world traveling around. You could have come here in plain clothes on your own. I'd have paid your fare. This way you may not have cost me money, but you've made me suffer the pains of the damned, and my pains aren't yet over. Perhaps it gives you some pleasure to travel at the expense of the Soviet Union. . . ."

Don Camillo shook his head.

"I didn't want to see the Soviet Union as a tourist. I wanted to see it through your eyes. It's one thing to see a show from the audience and another to be behind the scenes with the extras. Unless the Party has completely addled your brain you must know that I was on the level."

Peppone got up and went over to the stand where his suitcase was lying. He started to open it but stopped half-way.

"You've even taken my brandy!" he exclaimed. "What were you after when you insisted on giving it to Comrade Oregov, I'd like to know?"

"Nothing," said Don Camillo. "It was my loss as well as yours, because now I have to give you some of mine."

He produced his own bottle, and after swallowing a glassful Peppone was once more able to cope with the situation.

"Now then," said Don Camillo, once more showing him the two sheets of paper, "what do you propose to do?"

"Take care of it yourself," said Peppone. "I don't want to hear anything about it."

Don Camillo went straight to Gibetti's room. There he tackled the thorny matter without delay.

"Comrade Scamoggia has bad news, but he couldn't bear to tell it to you himself, so I'm here to tell you."

Gibetti leaped up from the bed where he lying.

"You may as well forget about that girl," said Don Camillo. "She's married and has five children."

"It can't be true!" said Gibetti.

"Comrade, you know Russian, don't you?" said Don Camillo.

"No."

"Then how did you manage to fraternize with her so closely?"

"We understood each other without words."

"And how did you manage to write to her?"

"I knew how to write her name and the name of her village, and I got someone to teach me how to say: 'I'm still thinking of you. I'll be back. Write me a letter.' And she had my address."

Don Camillo pulled the typewritten Russian sheet out of his pocket.

"Here's the report from her native place. You can get someone to translate it for you and you'll find in it everything I've been saying."

Gibetti looked searchingly at the letter.

"Her name and the name of the village are there, all right," he admitted.

"And so is the rest of what I told you," said Don Camillo. "In case you don't believe me, you can easily enough check on it when you get home."

Gibetti folded the paper and tucked it into his pocket.

"I shan't do anything of the sort," he replied. "I trust you completely. Next time I lose my head over a woman I'll just look at this paper and find a quick cure." He smiled sadly and went on: "Comrade, you know my Party record, don't you? Well, I did what I did, and many things I shouldn't have done as well, chiefly for the purpose of getting myself to Russia and looking for the girl. How am I to behave from now on?"

"Go right on fighting for the Cause."

"But my cause was Sonia and now someone else has taken it over."

Don Camillo shrugged his shoulders.

"Think it through, Comrade, that's all I can say. I've talked to you not as a Party comrade but as a friend. In my Party capacity, I know nothing of the whole affair."

"I do, though, to my sorrow," mumbled Gibetti as he threw himself back onto the bed.

The group met over the dinner table, all except for Gibetti, who was sick at his stomach. Comrade Oregov was in good spirits, because the afternoon program had gone off well. Comrade Bacciga was sitting beside Don Camillo, and managed to whisper in his ear:

"Comrade, I've made my deal. I exchanged my money and bought another mink stole."

"But how are you going to get it through the customs back home?" asked Don Camillo. "You can't very well pass off a mink stole as part of your personal linen."

"I'll sew it onto my overcoat collar. Plenty of men's overcoats are trimmed with fur. By the way, our reactionary press was, as usual, in error."

"I don't doubt it," said Don Camillo. "But what's the connection?"

"You told me that, according to the rate of exchange quoted by the reactionary papers, I'd get twenty rubles for every dollar. But I got twenty-six."

The vodka was going around and the conversation grew more and more gay.

"Comrade Tarocci," said Scamoggia, "it's a shame you couldn't come with us. A visit to the tomb of Lenin is something never to be forgotten."

"Quite right," said Comrade Curullu, who was sitting nearby. "To see the last resting-place of Stalin makes a tremendous impression."

The mention of Stalin was not exactly tactful, and Don Camillo hastened to fill in the awkward silence that followed.

"Of course," he said diplomatically. "I remember how impressed I was by the tomb of Napoleon in Paris. And Napoleon is a pigmy alongside Lenin."

But Comrade Curullu, fortified by vodka, would not stand for a change of subject.

"Stalin, that's the great man," he said gloomily.

"Well spoken, Comrade," chimed in Comrade Li Friddi. "Stalin is the outstanding hero of Soviet Russia. Stalin won the war."

Comrade Curullu downed another glass of vodka.

"Today, in the line of workers waiting to visit the tomb, there were some American tourists. The girls were dressed as if they were going to a preview of a Marilyn Monroe picture. Little idiots, I call them!"

"Quite right, Comrade," Li Friddi assented. " I was just as disgusted as you. Moscow isn't Capri or Monte Carlo."

"If Stalin were still alive, those little idiots wouldn't have been allowed to enter the country. Stalin had the capitalists scared to death."

Peppone, with the aid of Comrade Nadia Petrovna, was doing his best to distract Comrade Oregov's attention. But at a certain point Comrade Oregov pricked up his ears and demanded a translation of what was being said at the other end of the table. Peppone sent a mute S.O.S. signal to Don Camillo.

"Comrades," Don Camillo said gravely to the two recalcitrants, "nobody denies the merits of Stalin. But this is neither the time nor the place to speak of them."

"Truth knows neither time nor place!" Comrade Curullu insisted. "Even if today the Soviet Union has conquered the moon, the truth is that the Party has lost the revolutionary inspiration for which two hundred and fifty thousand men laid down their lives."

"Policies have to be adapted to the circumstances of the moment," Don Camillo timidly objected. "The end is what counts, not the means."

"The fact is that Stalin got everything he wanted without bothering to set foot outside the Soviet Union," insisted Curullu.

Don Camillo relapsed into silence and let the vodka take over. Little by little, all the comrades, except for Peppone, were overcome by nostalgia for Stalin. Peppone sat with clenched jaws, waiting for the inevitable explosion. Comrade Oregov confabulated excitedly with Comrade Nadia Petrovna and then leaped to his feet, pounding with his fist on the table. His eyes were feverishly bright and he was pale as a ghost. There was an icy silence until he shouted in strangely accented but comprehensible Italian:

"Long live Stalin!"

He raised his glass, and the others leaped to their feet and followed suit.

"Hurrah!" they shouted all together.

Comrade Oregov drained his glass and the rest of them did the same. Then he dashed it to the floor and they did likewise. Comrade Nadia Petrovna abruptly announced:

"Comrade Oregov wishes his Italian comrades a very good night."

The party broke up, in silence. Don Camillo and Peppone were the last to leave the private dining room, and Comrade Nadia Petrovna blocked their way.

"Comrades," she said, "may I offer you a cup of coffee?"

They stared at her, perplexed.

"It will be brewed in Italian style," she explained, smiling. "My house is only a short distance away."

Behind the ancient palaces and the American-style skyscrapers lay a proletarian section of the city. Comrade Petrovna lived on the fourth floor of a shabby house whose stairways reeked of cabbage and cooking oil. Her apartment consisted of a single room, furnished with two couches, a table, four chairs, a wardrobe and a stand for the radio. The curtains at the windows, some tasselled lampshades and the rug on the floor were obviously meant to be decorative, but did little to alleviate the bleakness of the surroundings.

"This is the comrade with whom I live," she said, introducing the girl who had opened the door. Although the girl was older, stockier and more rustic in appearance than Comrade Petrovna she was obviously cut from the same cloth. "She's an interpreter of French, but she speaks a fair amount of Italian as well," Comrade Petrovna added.

The coffee was already brewing over an alcohol burner in the middle of the table.

"We make it here," Comrade Petrovna explained, "because we share a kitchen with the next apartment, and it's across the hall." The flavor was unexpectedly delicious, and the two girls were gratified by their guests' appreciation. "I hope you're enjoying your trip to our great country," said Comrade Petrovna when the compliments were over.

Peppone, who was in a jovial mood, launched into an enthusiastic recapitulation of the wonders of the journey. But Comrade Petrovna's friend cut him short.

"We know all these things," she said. "Talk to us about Italy."

"Comrades," said Peppone, throwing out his arms in mock despair, "Italy is a small country, which might be a wonderful place to live in if it weren't infested with capitalists and clergy."

"But there's a good bit of freedom, isn't there?" put in Comrade Petrovna.

"On the surface the country is free," answered Peppone. "But the priests are secretly in control and they have spies everywhere. By the time we get home they will know every detail of our travels."

"Really?" said the other girl.

"You can tell her better than I," said Peppone, turning to Don Camillo.

"It's the truth," admitted Don Camillo. "I can swear to it."

"How terrible!" exclaimed Comrade Petrovna.

"And how does the average worker get along? Comrade Scamoggia, for instance?"

"Scamoggia isn't an average unskilled worker," Peppone explained. "He's an expert mechanic with a busy workshop of his own."

"Approximately how much money does he make?" she asked with an apparently casual air.

"If you figure thirty liras to the ruble, then he makes about seven hundred rubles a month," said Peppone after a quick mental calculation.

The two girls exchanged a few words in Russian together and then Comrade Petrovna went on:

"It all depends on the purchasing power of the lira. How much does it cost, in rubles, to buy a man's suit or a pair of shoes?"

"That varies, according to the quality," put in Don Camillo. "A suit may cost anywhere between seven and fourteen hundred rubles; a pair of shoes anywhere from seventy to three hundred and fifty."

"What about the suit you are wearing?" asked Comrade Petrovna's roommate of Peppone, fingering its luxurious senatorial fabric.

"Forty thousand liras," he replied.

"That's about one thousand three hundred and fifty rubles," interpolated Don Camillo.

"But to return to Scamoggia," said Peppone, "I repeat that he's a special case. Scamoggia. . . ."

"Scamoggia, Scamoggia!" exclaimed the roommate. "I'm

always hearing that name. Is he the individual who behaved so dreadfully at the Tifiz *kolkhos?* I don't see how such a fellow can keep on belonging to the Party."

"He's not a bad fellow at all," said Peppone. "You mustn't judge him from appearances. He's a sharp-witted and loyal Party man."

"Perhaps his parents were unenlightened and didn't bring him up the right way."

"No, there's nothing wrong with his family. You have to know Rome to understand him. When Roman men are away from home, they put on a devil-may-care air. But within their own four walls they don't dare open their mouths for fear of their wives."

"Is Scamoggia afraid of his wife?" the roommate inquired.

"Not yet. He hasn't got one," said Peppone, laughing. "But once he's married he'll be like all the rest."

Comrade Nadia Petrovna came back into the conversation with a question about Italian citrus-fruit production, which Peppone answered with a volley of statistics. She listened attentively and insisted on serving a second cup of coffee. Then she offered to guide the two men back to the hotel, but they insisted that they could find it alone. On the way, Peppone remarked that few Italian women had achieved such political maturity as that of Comrade Nadia Petrovna and her friend.

"Can you imagine one of our girls interested in heavy industry and fruit production in the Soviet Union?"

"No, I can't," said Don Camillo with a dead-pan expression. "An Italian girl is interested only in the young man who's courting her. She wants to make sure he isn't married, to find out about his family background, salary and reputation."

Peppone came to a sudden halt, as if some suspicion were crossing his mind.

"Are you insinuating that. . . ."

"I'm insinuating nothing," retorted Don Camillo. "No Communist senator would come to Moscow as a marriage broker. He has more important things to do than to look out for pretty girls for his Party comrades."

"Quite right!" roared Peppone, oblivious of his companion's irony. "Pretty girls are far from my thoughts, and so are married women, in spite of the fact that my wife wants me to bring her back some furs just like her neighbor's."

This was obviously a sore point, and when he had got it off his chest he felt better. It was ten o'clock in the evening and an icy wind swept through the deserted streets. Moscow seemed like the capital of Soviet melancholy.

14

The Next-to-Last Wave

THEY LEFT MOSCOW for the airport by bus early in the morning, when there was no one to be seen except street cleaners. Young girls and middle-aged women were spraying the streets with water, running mechanical sweepers and brushing up what these left behind with brooms. Don Camillo pointed out to Peppone how their every gesture seemed to indicate pride in the privilege of doing a man's work.

"It's a comforting sight," he concluded, "and one you can't see anywhere except in the Soviet Union."

"I shall be still more comforted on the day when in our own country we conscript priests for this job," mumbled Peppone.

An icy wind which seemed to come straight from the tundras of Siberia blew, unimpeded, through the empty streets. Only in the vast Red Square did it find human targets. What looked like bundles of rags, waiting for the street cleaners to come and carry them away, revealed themselves on second glance to be pilgrims lined up for the ritual visit to the mausoleum. Peasants from Uzbekistan, Georgia, Irkutsk and other remote parts of Russia had been ousted from their trains in the middle of the night and now sat, huddled together like sheep, on their suitcases, until such time as the approach to the tomb should be opened.

141

"Comrade," said Don Camillo, "how different this is from the days when poor mujiks traveled in wagons to St. Petersburg and and camped out for days in the park until they had a chance to see the Tsar and his German bride."

"It's one thing to be a slave performing an act of submission to a tyrant and another to be a free citizen paying tribute to his liberator," Peppone retorted.

"Besides the fact that many of them come to make sure of the fact that Lenin and Stalin are really dead."

Peppone smiled blandly.

"When I think that by midnight tomorrow I shall be unloading the lot of you at the Milan railway station, I have to pinch myself to be sure it isn't a dream. Enjoy your fun while you can. The time is running out. . . ."

The adventure was nearly over. At nine o'clock the plane would disembark them at S., where they were to visit a shipyard, then they were to travel for three hours by boat to the city of O. and board another plane for Berlin. The boat trip was Comrade Oregov's idea. Planes, trains, buses, trolleys and subways had all contributed to a demonstration of Soviet efficiency in the field of transportation, but a voyage by sea was necessary to complete it. Comrade Oregov had submitted his final project to the higher-ups and was visibly proud that it had been accepted.

Punctually at nine o'clock the plane landed at S. The airfield was small, commensurate with the size of the town, which had no importance except for its shipyard. In the broad, well-defended harbor, equipped for all possible repairs, there were ships of every description. Comrade Bacciga of Genoa felt immediately at home and was more loquacious than he had ever shown himself before. Among the various craft there was a gleaming new tanker and he described its tonnage and fittings with such familiarity and technical skill that Comrade Oregov felt his guidance was quite unnecessary. He left the little group of Italians in

Comrade Nadia Petrovna's charge and went off to the shipyard to arrange the details of the visit.

Comrade Bacciga was in top form. He had a ready answer to every question and exclaimed at intervals:

"Shipbuilding is a Genoese specialty, but these fellows are experts and I take off my hat to them."

Don Camillo was on the alert, and after Bacciga had several times announced this opinion he said:

"They're experts, all right, and from away back. Just look at that old schooner! Isn't it a beauty?"

The others followed Don Camillo along the quay until they came to a place where the schooner was in full view. It seemed to be straight out of a nineteenth-century engraving, and yet a fresh coat of paint and varnish made it look at the same time brand-new.

"It's wonderful what respect the Russians have for everything that harks back to their glorious past!" Don Camillo exclaimed. "Comrades, this ship bears witness to a long and noble tradition." Then, after a few minutes of silent admiration, he turned to Bacciga. "Comrade longshoreman, for centuries we have been masters of the art of shipbuilding, but to see a schooner like this we had to come all the way to the Soviet Union."

Comrade Nadia Petrovna had gleaned further information from one of the workers.

"*Tovarisch* is the ship's name," she informed them. "It's used for cadet training."

"Three thousand tons," put in Comrade Bacciga, turning suddenly upon her. "It was originally called the *Cristoforo Colombo* and was a training ship of the Italian Navy."

Comrade Petrovna blushed.

"Forgive me, Comrade," she muttered. Then, because she had caught sight of Comrade Oregov, walking toward them in the company of a shipyard official, she went to receive instructions. Peppone tugged at Don Camillo's sleeve and drew him apart from the others.

"Can't you keep that big mouth of yours shut?" he whispered. "Now you've made a real blunder."

"It wasn't a blunder at all," said Don Camillo. "I knew all along that it was the *Cristoforo Colombo*. I'll never forget how badly I felt the day when they took it and the *Giulio Cesare* away."

Comrade Bacciga was standing nearby and Peppone turned to vent his ire on him.

"Couldn't *you* have shut up about it?"

"How could I, Chief?" said Bacciga. "I recognized it from the start."

"A loyal Party member wouldn't have allowed himself any such recognition."

"I may be a loyal Party member, but don't forget that I'm also a professional longshoreman," Bacciga retorted.

"What do you mean by that?"

"Water's water everywhere," said Bacciga, "but there's a big difference between the sea and the Po River. I can't look at the *Cristoforo Colombo* with as little emotion as if it were a river barge."

"The sailors of the famous cruiser *Potemkin* weren't of the same stamp as you," said Peppone sarcastically.

"But then they weren't Genoese," siad Bacciga.

At eleven o'clock, with their heads crammed full of statistics, the Italians finished their tour of the shipyard. Their ship was not due to leave for another hour, and while Comrade Nadia Petrovna took the main body of the group to look at the town, Comrade Oregov, Peppone and Don Camillo went to have a drink in a workers' canteen. Comrade Oregov worked on a report of the day's activities, while the other two fortified their spirits for the coming sea voyage. A bitter wind and a mass of clouds in the sky seemed to foretell a storm.

The canteen was ill-lit and dirty, but it served excellent

vodka. After the second round Peppone confided to Don Camillo:

"I'm afraid of being seasick. How about you?"

"Not in the least. Priests have been storm-tossed for nearly two thousand years, and they've always managed to come out alive."

"We'll see if you can still crack jokes when we're on the high seas," said Peppone.

Soon the cold wind drove the rest of the group indoors. They didn't look as if they had had much fun, and the dourest of them all was Comrade Curullu. After they had all sat down and a glass of vodka had loosened their tongues, Comrade Curullu proceeded to let off steam.

"Do you know where we have been, Comrade?" he asked Don Camillo.

Don Camillo put away his book of excerpts from Lenin.

"In a church!" Curullu continued. "And do you know what was going on?"

Don Camillo shrugged his shoulders.

"A wedding!" said Curullu excitedly. "Complete with priest and all the usual rubbish!" And he added, turning to Comrade Scamoggia: "And to think that you came here in the hope that there'd be no priests cluttering up the landscape! You should have seen this one! He was sleek and well fed and rigged out in even fancier vestments than ours. And the bride and groom! There they were, all dressed up, with their hands folded in prayer and a sickly, angelic smile on their faces! It was enough to make your stomach turn over."

"A disgusting sight to see in the Soviet Union!" chimed in Comrade Li Friddi. "You'd have thought we were in a backward village in Sicily."

They all looked expectantly at Don Camillo, and he had a ready reply.

"Comrades, the Soviet constitution allows every citizen to practice his own personal religion. And as long as the priests don't corrupt young people under eighteen years of age with their teachings, they are free to exercise their trade. This is nothing so very startling. The whole story of religious persecution is Vatican propaganda."

Comrade Oregov had pricked up his ears and with the aid of Comrade Nadia Petrovna was following the conversation. Don Camillo looked to him for a sign and he hastened to respond.

"He says that Comrade Tarocci is quite right," said Comrade Petrovna. "Paragraph 124 of the Constitution is observed to the letter. The Council for the Orthodox Church and the Council for Religious Bodies see to it that there is complete freedom of conscience; in fact they help the churches solve practical problems."

"That makes it perfectly clear," said Don Camillo. "The priests don't do whatever they please, as they do at home; they do only what the Constitution allows. It's quite a different situation."

"But it adds up to the same thing," protested Comrade Li Friddi. "Priests are priests, wherever you find them."

Don Camillo laughed.

"Comrade, in this enormous country there are only twenty-six thousand churches and thirty-five thousand clergy."

"That's too many of both," muttered Comrade Curullu.

"Remember that in 1917 there were forty-six thousand churches and fifty thousand priests, and in 1945 there were only four thousand churches and five thousand priests," said Don Camillo.

"Is that true?" Comrade Curullu asked incredulously, turning to Comrade Oregov.

After the usual translation Comrade Nadia Petrovna replied on his behalf:

"Those figures are substantially correct. Today priests and their churches receive no money except from their parishioners. During the war the Orthodox Church gave full patriotic support to the war effort. And the Party uses nonviolent, dissuasive means to combat superstition."

But vodka caused Comrade Curullu to give further vent to his disillusionment.

"Comrade," he said to Comrade Petrovna, "if in the last fourteen years the number of priests has grown from five thousand to thirty-five thousand, how can you say that there has been a combat against superstition?"

Comrade Petrovna hesitated a moment before relaying this question to Comrade Oregov, and he listened to her with a bowed head, as if he were personally responsible for this betrayal. Finally he looked up and threw out his arms in despair. There was no need for Comrade Nadia Petrovna to translate for him. This was the end of the discussion. Comrade Oregov returned to working over his report and the visitors spoke of other things. The canteen was filled with smoke, and Don Camillo felt a need of fresh air. He went out onto the street, and Peppone followed after. The wind had died down and they were able to stroll quietly up and down, side by side. Finally Peppone exclaimed:

"Thirty-five thousand priests. After a bloody revolution and thirty-two years of sacrifice on behalf of the people!"

"Don't get excited, Comrade," said Don Camillo soothingly. "Numbers shouldn't alarm you. These Russian priests are only government employees. They call the Pope an enemy of peace, and their old Patriarch Alexis once referred to Stalin as having been 'sent by God.' But although Communism has won over the priests it has lost the war against religion. And it has lost two other wars: the war against the peasants and the war against the *bourgeoisie*. After four decades of struggle the Soviet Union has gained atomic supremacy and conquered the moon; it has installed science in the place of superstition and subjugated both its own people and the peoples of the satellite nations; it has killed off ten million peasants in the process of agricultural reform and eliminated the old middle class. Yet today, in their

search for God, the Russians are spending their hard-earned
rubles to build churches. Agricultural production is below
the pre-revolutionary level and the government has been
forced to allow the peasants to have a portion of privately
owned land and to sell its produce on the free market. At
the same time there is a new and increasingly powerful
bourgeoisie. Don't take offense, Comrade, but you yourself,
with your well-tailored, double-breasted dark blue suit, the
two salaries which you receive as a senator and a Party
leader, your bank account and your intention of buying a
high-powered car, are a budding bourgeois. Can you deny
it?"

"What do you mean, a 'high-powered car'? I'm going to
buy a second-hand standard model."

Don Camillo shook his head.

"It isn't the horsepower that counts; it's the principle of
the thing."

Peppone took a leather case out of his pocket and extracted a big Tuscan-type cigar. Don Camillo, who for the
past two days had been longing for the familiar aroma,
heaved a formidable sigh and said bitterly:

"There you are! The *bourgeoisie* feast while the people
are famished!"

Angrily Peppone broke the cigar in two and offered half
of it to Don Camillo.

"Thirty-five thousand priests weren't enough," he muttered; "you had to come and join them!"

At this moment they heard the ship whistle.

The *Partisan* was a light but powerful and up-to-date
craft, which ploughed steadily and speedily through the
water. The first hour of the voyage left nothing to be de-
sired. Unfortunately the devil intervened; the sky darkened
again and the wind began to blow. In order that the giant
waves should not throw the ship onto the rocky shore, the
captain steered farther out to sea in search of calmer

weather. But the storm only increased in intensity and soon the ship was dangerously drifting. A sailor came down into the saloon and hurled a pile of canvas objects on the floor.

"The captain says to put on the life jackets and go up on deck," said Comrade Nadia Petrovna.

On deck all hell seemed to have broken loose. Rain poured down from the sky and waves beat mercilessly against the sides of the ship. The sky was pitch-black and the wind was howling. The wheel rotated wildly and two lifeboats were swept away. All eyes were turned on the captain, who stood clinging to the rail of the bridge. He knew that all those present were looking to him for safety, but he avoided their gaze and stared helplessly out over the water. How long would the ship hold together? A giant wave lifted the stern and it seemed as if the bow would sink into the sea. After the wave had broken over the deck and the ship had regained its balance, the passengers looked around and counted their numbers. They were all there: Peppone and his group, Comrade Oregov and Comrade Petrovna, the captain and the six members of the crew. Huddled together, holding on to whatever object came to hand, they had miraculously survived the first inundation. But how would they manage to survive another? The ship slid along the side of the next wave and down into the hollow. Then it came to the surface again, but one of the portholes was shattered and the hold began to fill with water. Hopelessly Peppone turned to Don Camillo:

"For the love of God, do something!" he shouted.

Don Camillo summoned all his self-control.

"Lord," he said, "I am happy to die in Your service."

Forgetful of where he was and of the fact that none of his companions except Peppone knew him except under the name of Comrade Tarocci, he bared his head and reached into his pocket for the crucifix concealed in a fountain pen. He held it up over their heads and they fell onto their knees before him, even Comrade Petrovna, the captain and the crew. Only Comrade Oregov kept his cap pulled down over his eyes and clung to the stairway which led to the bridge, looking at the sight with amazement.

"Lord," Don Camillo prayed, "have mercy on Your unfortunate children. . . ."

As he spoke a wave dashed against the side of the ship and another threatened to break over the deck.

"*Ego vos absolvo a peccatis vestris, in nomine Patris et Filii et Spiritus Sancti. . . .*"

He traced a sign of the cross in the stormy air, and his hearers crossed themselves and crept forward to kiss the crucifix. A mountain of water broke over the deck, but God had other designs for them and did not allow it to sweep them away. They rose to their feet, suddenly confident that the worst was over. All of them had noticed that Comrade Oregov had neither taken off his cap nor fallen to his knees, but only now did they mentally question the consequences. He was standing stock-still, with clenched jaws and blazing eyes. Comrade Nadia Petrovna, the captain and the members of the crew were alarmed by his menacing stare, but the Italians were so happy to be alive they paid no attention.

The ship was still shaken by the storm, but the sailors were able to man the pumps while the passengers went to wring out their drenched clothes. Comrade Oregov's attitude was quickly forgotten. As the storm gradually subsided shipboard life returned to normal. Two hours later men were talking among themselves just as they did every day. After all, nothing so very extraordinary had happened. A heavy sea, decks awash with water, a shattered porthole, two lifeboats swept away—the everyday occurrences of a sea voyage. No one thought of Comrade Oregov until the ship reached port and Comrade Nadia Petrovna mentioned his name. The gangplank was in place and

Peppone and his group were about to walk down it when Comrade Nadia Petrovna planted herself in their way.

"We must wait for Comrade Oregov," she said with a tremor in her voice.

Just then the captain came along and led her away below deck. He brought her back a few minutes later and smilingly shook Don Camillo's hand.

"*Kak trevòga, tak do Bòga,*" he said.

"We can disembark," Comrade Petrovna explained. "Unfortunately one of the last waves carried Comrade Oregov away. The Party has lost an able and devoted servant. A valiant soldier is dead."

When they set foot on land, Don Camillo looked anxiously out to sea, half-expecting to see the ghost of Comrade Oregov between the lowering clouds and the storm-tossed water.

"May God forgive you your sins!" he said to himself, trying to convince himself of the truth of the captain's story. If the captain had written in his log that two lifeboats and Comrade Oregov had been lost at sea, what reason was there to doubt him?

The departure of the Berlin plane was delayed by the storm. In the bus which carried them to the airfield Don Camillo found himself sitting across from Comrade Scamoggia.

"Well, Comrade," he said, "the time has come to say good-by. You'll be staying on after we have gone away."

"No, I'm going with you," Scamoggia replied.

"Wasn't Comrade Petrovna able to persuade you to stay?"

"I never even mentioned the possibility. I feel I'm still needed by the Italian Communist Party."

"Very good, Comrade! A Party stalwart must subordinate love to duty."

Comrade Scamoggia sighed and looked out the window.

The bus came to a stop at the arifield gate and they all got out. Comrade Nadia Petrovna and Peppone went into the office with the group's traveling papers. The police official glanced over them and passed on the list of names to his interpreter, who proceeded to call them out one by one.

"Pietro Bacciga. . . ."

Bacciga came in, and both Peppone and Comrade Petrovna confirmed his identity. When his name had been checked, Comrades Capece, Gibetti, Li Friddi and Peratto followed.

"Walter Rondella. . . ."

Peppone forgot that Comrade Rondella had been ignominiously shipped back home. He looked up and saw the Neapolitan barber whom they had met at the Tifiz *kolkhos* standing brazenly before him. Already he had approved the fellow's name as that of Rondella and Comrade Petrovna had assented. When Comrade Tarocci was called in Peppone was tempted to disavow him. But this vengeful impulse had no time to take root in his mind.

"Ten entries, ten exits," said the interpreter, as he handed the papers back to Peppone.

As they walked toward the plane Don Camillo asked Comrade Petrovna to tell him the exact meaning of the Russian words which the ship captain had pronounced at the moment of disembarkment.

"He was summing up what happened during the storm," she replied. " 'In dire extremity man remembers his God.' "

"An outdated Russian proverb," muttered Don Camillo.

As the travelers climbed into the plane Comrade Petrovna shook hands with them, one by one. When it came to the Neapolitan barber, who was also a refugee from Rumania, it was all she could do to contain her laughter. But the sight of Comrade Scamoggia froze the smile on her lips. Don Camillo was the last to climb aboard.

"Good-by," he said.

"Pray for me, Comrade," Comrade Petrovna whispered, and there were tears rolling down her cheeks.

For a long time after the plane had left the ground Don Camillo could not stop thinking of the sorrowful expression in her eyes. Then he looked down at the endless expanse of mist-covered fields and remembered a Russian phrase which he had jotted down in his notebook: "*Spasitjel mira, spasi Rossiu!*—Savior of the world, save Russia!"

15

A Story That Has No End

LORD," SAID DON CAMILLO to the crucified Christ above the altar, "for two whole weeks I've been back in my own familiar surroundings, and I still can't get over the feeling of distress from which I suffered during my travels. Mind You, Lord, it was distress, not fear; I had no reason to be afraid. I was deeply ashamed, like an old soldier, used to fighting out in the open, when he finds himself under false colors, charged with penetrating the enemy ranks in order to plot their destruction. The crucifix concealed in a fountain pen, the breviary masked as a volume of excerpts from Lenin, the clandestine Masses celebrated before a bedside table . . . !"

"Don't torment yourself, Don Camillo," Christ answered gently. "You weren't a coward, trying to knife his neighbor in the back; you were trying to help him. Would you refuse a dying man a drink of water if it were necessary to lower yourself to practice deceit in order to bring it to him? The heroism of a soldier of Christ is humility; his only enemy is pride. Blessed are the meek. . . ."

"Lord, you are speaking from a Cross that has all the glory of a throne, a throne which you won in open battle, without the humiliation of disguise. You never appeared to men in the likeness of the Devil. . . ."

"Don Camillo, didn't the Son of God humble himself when he consented to live like a man and die like a common criminal? Just look at your God, at His wounded sides and the ignominious crown of thorns on His head!"

"Lord, I am looking at You," insisted Don Camillo, "but I see only the divine light of Your supreme sacrifice. No light at all, not even the wavering flare of a match, illuminates the wretched figure of 'Comrade Don Camillo.'"

Christ smiled.

"What about the light you kindled in the eyes of the old peasant woman of Drevinec? And the candle you lit on the unmarked grave of a soldier whose family did not even have the satisfaction of knowing where he lay? Then think back to the storm at sea and the terror of your miserable companions at the thought that their last hour had come. When you held up your crucifix and asked God to forgive them their sins, did they ridicule the transformation of Comrade Tarocci into a priest of the Church? No, they fell down on their knees and tried to kiss that tiny figure with the collapsible arms. Haven't you ever wondered what got into them?"

"But, Lord, any other priest would have behaved the same way," murmured Don Camillo.

"Remember that only Peppone knew who you were. For all the others you were simply Comrade Tarocci. How do you explain their change of heart?"

Don Camillo threw out his arms. Only now did he realize what an incredible episode it had been.

"You see," said Christ, "that some light must have been shed by 'Comrade Don Camillo.'"

For most of the two weeks since his return Don Camillo had been trying to put his travel notes in order for the Bishop's perusal. It was no easy job, for although the Bishop was old and forgetful, he had very exacting notions of grammar.

Ever since they had said good-by at the Milan railway station, Don Camillo had had no news of Peppone. The Neapolitan barber had dropped out of the group in West Berlin; Comrade Tavan, with his three stalks of wheat, had left the train at Verona, and Don Camillo had gotten off, along with Comrade Bacciga and Comrade Peratto, at Milan.

"Shouldn't you travel with us as far as Parma or Reggio Emilia?" Scamoggia had asked him. But Don Camillo claimed to have urgent business in Milan. This was quite true because there he had left his cassock and he was in a hurry to recuperate it. Peppone had counted his little troop and just as Don Camillo was leaving the train he heard him shout gaily to Scamoggia:

"There are only six of us from now on. Take this money and buy six bottles of wine. I want to treat you."

Peppone's laughter continued to ring in his ears and he racked his brain to know what had caused it. On the evening of the fourteenth day after his homecoming Peppone himself turned up to give him an explanation. For a moment Don Camillo failed to recognize his old friend. He had left him wearing a double-breasted dark-blue suit, a white shirt and a gray silk tie, and now here he was in his outfit of times long gone by: a corduroy jacket, wrinkled trousers, a cap pulled down over the back of his head, a handkerchief knotted around his neck and a peasant's black wool cape over his shoulders. Don Camillo stared at him for some minutes and then shook his head.

"How silly of me to forget," he exclaimed, "that the representative of the working class has to carry his load in a senatorial suit in Rome and in the rig of a mayor in his native village. It must be hard lines for you to travel only at night. Won't you sit down?"

"I can say what I have to say standing up," grumbled Peppone. "I've come to pay my debt." He pulled a candle out of his pocket and put it down on Don Camillo's desk.

"This is to thank the Lord for having saved me from shipwreck."

" 'In dire extremity man remembers his God,' as the Russian sea captain said," answered Don Camillo. "Usually when the extremity is past he proceeds to forget Him. I congratulate you on your good memory."

"And this is to thank the Lord for saving me from a certain priest whom the Devil sent to torment me," added Peppone lugubriously, drawing forth another candle, a giant one, four feet long and eight inches in diameter.

Don Camillo's jaw dropped.

"I had it made to order," Peppone explained. "It's big, if you like, but if it were to really represent the danger of that priest it would have to be four times bigger."

"You flatter me," said Don Camillo. "A country priest doesn't really deserve such consideration."

"There are country priests more dangerous than the Pope in person," said Peppone. He threw a parcel and three letters onto the desk and added: "These were sent to me with the request that I turn them over to Comrade Tarocci. I don't like it, not a bit. I warn you that if I receive any more I shall burn them."

Don Camillo opened the parcel, which was full of photographs, and looked hastily at one of the letters, which was addressed in the same writing.

"They are. . . ." he began.

"I'm not sticking my nose into your business, Father," said Peppone.

"But they pertain to Comrade Tarocci, who as cell-leader is obliged to inform his superior. They are pictures sent by Comrade Peratto, and he says I am to do what I please with them. Look at this group, where we are in the front row together. Doesn't it interest you?"

Peppone snatched the picture, examined it, and said between clenched teeth:

"I hope you're not going to get me into any more trouble!"

"Don't worry, Senator. Comrade Peratto has sent another set, of a strictly unofficial nature, which he asks me to place without mentioning his name. The Party doesn't pay him very well and he wants to make a bit of money."

"Would you play a dirty trick like that?"

"It's up to you. What if we fail to give him satisfaction and he sends a picture that has me in it to a Party paper?"

Peppone lowered himself into a chair and wiped the perspiration from his forehead. While he looked through the pictures Don Camillo read the second letter and informed him of its contents.

"This one is from Comrade Tavan. He thanks me for my good advice and says it has done wonders for his mother. He has planted the three stalks of wheat and goes to look at them every day. 'If they were to wither,' he says, 'I'd feel that my brother was even more dead than before.' And he sends his best wishes to the Comrade Senator."

Peppone only grunted in reply.

The third letter was a very short one, enclosing some money.

"It's from Comrade Gibetti," said Don Camillo. "When he got home he began to wonder about the contents of the Russian letter which told the story of the girl with whom he was in love. Finally he got it translated and found that she was dead. He has sent me a thousand liras to say a Mass for her soul. I'm going to send back the money and tell him I'll say a Mass for her every month."

Peppone brought his fist down on the desk.

"Who the devil told these fellows that you were a priest?" he thundered. "That's what I'd like to know!"

"Nobody told them. They simply got the idea."

"But how did they get it?"

"It was a question of seeing the light," said Don Camillo. "Since I'm no electrician, I can't explain."

Peppone shook his head.

"Perhaps the fault is mine. Perhaps there on the ship my tongue slipped and I called you 'Father.' "

"I don't remember your doing any such thing."

Peppone showed him a picture in which Comrade Oregov occupied a prominent place.

"When I saw him for the last time," he said with bowed head, "the fury of the storm was over. How did it happen that a wave washed him into the sea? What happened up on deck after we had gone below?"

"Only God can say," said Don Camillo. "And He alone knows how often the poor fellow is in my thoughts."

Peppone gave a deep sigh and got up.

"Here are the pictures I'd choose," he said.

"Agreed," said Don Camillo. "And what am I to do with the candles?"

Peppone shrugged his shoulders.

"The big one can be for the escape from shipwreck," he muttered.

"That's what you said for the smaller," Don Camillo reminded him.

"The smaller can be for the escape of the priest," shouted Peppone, and he went away without saying goodby.

Don Camillo went over to the church. There was no candlestick large enough to contain the giant candle, but he managed to fit it into a big bronze vase. When he had put both candles on the altar and lit them Don Camillo said:

"Lord, Peppone is mindful of you."

"And of you, too, if I'm not mistaken," Christ replied.

When the Bishop had read Don Camillo's report, he sent for him.

"Now give me the whole story," he said.

Don Camillo talked for several hours uninterruptedly and when he had finished the Bishop exclaimed:

"It's incredible! Conversion of Comrade Tavan and Comrade Gibetti, liberation of a Neapolitan barber, communion given to the old Polish woman, the marriage of her daughter to an Italian veteran and the baptism of their six children, the veteran's confession and rehabilitation, a Mass for the Dead celebrated in a forgotten cemetery and the absolution given to eighteen persons in imminent danger of death! And besides this you became a cell leader. All in the space of six days in the territory of the anti-Christ! I can hardly believe it!"

"Your Grace, besides my word there are the photographs and the letters. And I have a senator for a witness."

"A senator!" groaned the old man. "Then the damage is irreparable."

Don Camillo looked bewildered.

"My son, can't you see that under these conditions I'll simply have to raise you to the rank of *monsignore*."

"*Domine, non sum dignus,*" he murmured, raising his eyes to heaven.

The Bishop shook his head.

"Just what I said myself, many years ago, but no one paid any attention. God be with you!"

In the month that followed, the Russian adventure ceased to occupy Don Camillo's mind. But one morning as he was coming out of the church he caught Smilzo pasting a poster on the rectory wall. He did not make his presence known but when Smilzo came down from the ladder and almost knocked him over, he asked:

"Comrade, what if someone were to tear down your poster while the paste is still fresh and ram it down your throat?"

"Father, no man alive would do a thing like that!" Smilzo replied.

"Just suppose such a man *is* alive and standing here before you!"

He had taken hold of the lapels of Smilzo's ragged jacket and seemed to have no intention of letting them go.

"All right. . . . That would be a very different situation."

Don Camillo went on in a different tone:

"Look here; do I ever stick up posters on your 'People's Palace'? Why do you have to inflict your political idiocies on me?"

"This isn't politics," said Smilzo. "It's the announcement of a cultural event."

Without releasing his grip on Smilzo's jacket Don Camillo looked up and read a notice to the effect that Senator Giuseppe Bottazzi was to talk the following evening about his recent trip to the Soviet Union. A period of questions and answers would follow.

"You're right," he said, letting go of Smilzo's jacket. "It's a strictly cultural proposition. Where can I get a ticket?"

"Everybody's welcome and entrance is free," said Smilzo, straightening out his lapels. "And there are no holds barred on the questions."

"Even questions from me?"

"Even from the Bishop," said Smilzo, beating a cautious retreat. "We particularly want to educate the clergy."

He had retreated too far for Don Camillo to lay hands on him again, and besides the priest had other matters on his mind. He went into the rectory and picked up his pen. Half an hour later a boy delivered a letter to Peppone, which read as follows:

"*Dear Comrade Senator: I can hardly wait to come to tomorrow night's meeting. Just let me submit one advance question: Why are you looking for trouble? Best regards from—Comrade Tarocci."*

In the late afternoon Peppone was unexpectedly called to Rome and the next morning Smilzo had to add a postscript to the poster: *Because of the unavoidable absence of the speaker the meeting is postponed to an indefinite date.*

Once more, when he climbed down from the ladder, Smilzo found himself face to face with Don Camillo.

"Too bad!" said the priest. "Who knows how long the clergy will have to remain wrapped in the ignorance of the Dark Ages?"

Smilzo quickly picked up his ladder and retreated to a position of safety.

"Don't you worry, Father. We'll open their eyes!"

No later date was ever announced, and after rain had washed the poster away it received no further mention. Six months went by, and because Don Camillo had no opportunity of talking about his Russian trip he began to wonder whether it was all a dream. But one morning, when he was putting his papers in order, the sexton came to tell him that a stranger was at the door. To his utter amazement Don Camillo saw, over the sexton's shoulder, the face of Comrade Nanni Scamoggia.

"How did you get here?" he asked.

"There are such things as trains," said Scamoggia. "And I persuaded Comrade Bottazzi to give me your address."

"I see," said Don Camillo, although he didn't see at all. "What's the reason for your visit?"

Scamoggia was still the same devil-may-care fellow as before. This was quite plain from the way he lit his cigarette and threw himself into a chair. But his nonchalance did not deceive Don Camillo, who remembered the tears in Comrade Nadia Petrovna's eyes.

"I have a problem, Comrade. . . . I mean Father. It's that girl. . . ."

"Yes. What happened to her?"

"She came to Rome two months ago with a Russian women's delegation. When they left she cut loose and stayed behind."

"So what did you do?"

"In my Party position I couldn't have dealings with a traitor to the Soviet Union. . . ."

"So what next?"

"In order to marry her I had to leave the Party," said Scamoggia, tossing his cigarette butt into the fire.

"Is that the problem?"

"No, it's this. We've been married for a month now, and every day she says the civil ceremony isn't enough. She wants a church wedding."

"I don't see much to worry about," Don Camillo observed calmly.

"You wouldn't," said Scamoggia. "But don't forget that the very sight of a priest turns my stomach."

"I understand, Comrade. You have a right to your own opinions. But if that's the case, why have you come to me?"

"Because if a priest does have to be dragged into it, I'd rather he were a regular fellow. And you're a sort of ex-comrade, like myself. In fact, you're my former cell leader."

"Not a bad idea," said Don Camillo.

Scamoggia went to open the door and shouted:

"Nadia!"

A second later Comrade Petrovna entered the room. As soon as she saw Don Camillo, she rushed to kiss his hand.

"How revolting!" muttered Scamoggia. "So short a time in this country and she knows all the rules!"

All their papers were in good order and the marriage ceremony was a rapid affair. Peppone had to accept the job of giving the bride away. But he did it with a smile.

Before the couple went away Don Camillo took the girl aside and asked her to tell him the true story of Comrade Oregov.

"It was an ugly affair," she explained. "When the rest of us went below deck, Comrade Oregov ordered the captain to lock us all up and put handcuffs on you and Comrade Bottazzi. He raved about betrayal, and Vatican spies and commissions of inquiry. Finally he appeared to be quite mad. He and the captain came to blows and the captain knocked him against the rail. Just then a wave swept him away. This is the whole truth, but only the captain, you and I know it. It's all very sad. . . ."

After the bride and groom had left, Don Camillo and Peppone sat warming their hands at the fire in the study. For some time they were silent, and then Don Camillo exclaimed:

"I must jot that down before I forget it."

He pulled the famous notebook out of his pocket and said aloud as he was writing:

"Two more conversions and another marriage. . . ."

"Put down whatever you like," roared Peppone. "It will all go on your bill on the day of the Great Uprising!"

"Won't you give me a small discount?" asked Don Camillo. "I'm an ex-comrade, after all."

"We'll let you choose the place where you are to be hanged," jeered Peppone.

"I can tell you that right now," retorted Don Camillo. "Right beside you!"

It was a cold winter day and the mist rising from the river clouded over the end of this newly finished story, which already was older than time.

A Note from the Author

THIS BOOK—the latest of the series of *The Little World of Don Camillo*—was published in installments in the last fourteen issues (1959) of *Candido*, the Milanese weekly which I founded in 1945 and which played a propaganda role of recognized value in the important general election of 1948, when it contributed to the defeat of the Communist ticket.

Candido is no longer in existence. It suspended publication in 1962, chiefly because the Italians of the "economic miracle" and the "opening to the Left" have lost all interest in the anti-Communist struggle. The present generation of Italians is made up of "purists," that is, of conscientious objectors, anti-nationalists, and do-gooders. It grew up in the school of political corruption, of neorealist films and of the sexual-sociological literature of Left-wing writers. It is not a generation at all, but a degeneration.

What a wonderful place was the poverty-stricken Italy of 1945! We came back from the starvation of the Nazi prison camps to find our country a heap of rubble. But through the ruins in which so many innocent victims had died a fresh breeze of hope was blowing. What a difference there is between the material poverty of 1945 and the spiritual poverty of the newly rich of 1963! The wind that blows among the skyscrapers of the "economic miracle" stinks of sex and sewerage and death. In the prosperous *dolce-vita* Italy all hope of a better world is dead. There is only an unholy mixture of hell and holy water, as we face a new generation of priests who are no brothers of Don Camillo.

In the newly rich Red Italy *Candido* could not survive, and indeed it died. And the story which came out in installments in 1959, although it lives on because of the vitality of its characters, is out-of-date. Its essentially light-hearted quarrel with Communism is understandable only in the light of the time at which it was written.

The reader may at this point object: "If the attitude toward Communism has changed and your story is out-of-date, then why didn't you bury it in the tomb of *Candido*?" To which I reply: "Because some few people have not changed their attitude and I have an obligation of loyalty toward them."

I dedicate my story to the American soldiers who died in Korea, the last brave defenders of the besieged West, to them and to their dear ones, who have some reason to hold to their opinions.

Likewise I dedicate it to the Italian soldiers who died in Russia and to the sixty-three thousand of them who were shut up in Soviet prison-camps and of whose fate nothing is known. To them in particular I dedicate the chapter entitled *Three Stalks of Wheat*.

I dedicate it further to the three hundred priests who were assassinated by the Communists in the province of Emilia during the bloody days of Italy's "liberation," and to the late Pope Pius XII, who blasted Communists and their accomplices. And to the Primate of Hungary, the indomitable Cardinal Mindszenty and to the heroically martyred Church of his country. To all of these I dedicate the chapter entitled *Christ's Secret Agent*.

The last chapter, *A Story That Has No End*, I dedi-

cate to the late Pope John XXIII. This is not only
obvious reasons but also (if the reader will forgive me)
for a motive of a very personal nature. After Pope John
died in June 1963, the statements issued by public figures
the world over included one from Vincent Auriol, the
socialist president of France when Pope John was Apostolic
Nuncio to Paris. In this statement Auriol said (and I quote
him verbatim): "On New Year's Day of 1952, mindful of
my disputes with the mayor and the parish priest of my
town, he sent me as a present a book by Guareschi, *The
Little World of Don Camillo,* with these words on the
flyleaf: 'To Monsieur Vincent Auriol, president of the
French Republic, for his amusement and for his spiritual
profit, from J. Roncalli, Apostolic Nuncio.' "

The Don Camillo of 1959 is the same as the Don Camillo
of 1952, and I have written this story—even if it is out of
date—for the "amusement" and (forgive my heavy-handed-
ness) for the "spiritual profit" of the few friends I have
left in the disjointed world of today.

Giovanni Guareschi

Roncole-Verdi, August 16, 1963

golfers' gold

AN INSIDER'S VIEW OF PRO GOLF AND PRO GOLFERS— PALMER, NICKLAUS, PLAYER, SNEAD, VENTURI AND MANY OTHERS—BY

"champagne tony" lema

WITH
GWILYM S. BROWN

50110 / 50¢

If your bookseller does not have this title, you may order it by sending retail price, plus 10¢ for mailing and handling to: MAIL SERVICE DEPARTMENT, Pocket Books, Inc., 1 West 39th Street, New York, New York 10018. Not responsible for orders containing cash. Please send check or money order.

PUBLISHED BY POCKET BOOKS, INC.